Iron Heart
Jemma's Story
Book 1

E.C.Yoho

(Iron Heart-Jemma's Story) Copyright © 2023
E.C.Yoho

This book is a work of fiction. Names, characters, places, and incidents are the product of the author's imagination or are used fictitiously. Any resemblance to actual events, locales, or persons, living or dead, is coincidental.

All rights reserved. No part of this book may be reproduced or transmitted in any form or by any means without written permission from the author.

Edited by Bambi Sommers

Cover by E.C.Yoho

For my dad, who left us too soon.

INTRO

The war to end all wars, or at least that is what they called it. No matter where you went, walls in every city were plastered with propaganda showing men and woman in uniforms, smiling and grouped together as though it was a family photo. All of them having captions with sayings such as "We want you!" or "Enlist today!"

Not one citizen seemed to notice that some of the people who decided to join the war efforts never came back. While those who did return acted as though they were in a constant fog, effects caused by the war according to medical personnel. In fact, if you ever came across one you may have known, you would not recognize them. The person they once were and everything they once believed and stood for was gone. Nothing more than shells of their former selves, they often resembled those zombies from movies and television shows, minus eating brains and chasing people of course. But zombies, none the less.

Soon a rumor spread saying those who "enlisted" were being subjected to some form of medical testing, and the government was making an army of super soldiers. Even if the rumors were true, all accusations of super soldiers were silenced by "no comment" replies, and shut down before they could go any farther. Everyone was being assured no such experiments were being done on humans now or ever and, to really throw everyone off, they also questioned all the citizens by asking "if super soldiers exist, why has no one seen their existence yet?"

My twin sister, Alise, and I were born in a small town on the northern outskirts of Denver, Colorado; a town that barely seemed to exist when its place was in the long shadow of Denver. It was like most small towns, where everyone knew everyone, as well as a place where nothing ever happened.

Well, that was all prior to the war going unforgivably in the wrong direction.

Lillian McKnight, our mother, always told Alise and myself we were special, we were like no one else in the whole world. I am not sure if that was the real reason the army seemed interested in us, but I had always longed to get more answers about why the two of us were so special. Why choose to come after us?

The army had first sent their recruiters to talk to Lillian shortly after we had our fifth birthday, begging her to let them take Alise and me with them to a facility, explaining it was of grave importance. "It could help save not just America, but the world." Even with all the talking in the world, she constantly turned them away. "No matter how much you beg me for them, you will never take my girls from me."

They began to get desperate as the years went on and, having been refused what they wanted for eight long years, they were beginning to lose their patience with Lillian McKnight. Knowing the time for talking rationally to our mother was over, they sent the one person on the planet who could possibly convince her to give us to them.

CHAPTER 1

The sun shines brightly as it begins to warm up the ground quickly this August morning. Alise and I sit outside under the tall pine tree in our back yard, enjoying the calming effect of the wind rustling through the leaves. As we are talking, we cannot help but believe the day is going to be perfect. With the birds happily singing their songs as they fly by, there was absolutely nothing that could possibly go wrong.

All the joyous thoughts fade as we watch a black SUV drive past our back yard and out of sight as it pulls into our driveway. The peaceful day is disturbed by the crunching of tires rolling slowly over the rocks in the driveway at the front of the house.

Alise and I look at one another before standing up to get a quick glance of a well-dressed young man as he gets out of the passenger side. We decide he looks about eighteen as he walks up the dirt path that leads to our house's front door. He turns to look in our direction and we quickly duck behind the house so he does not spot us. The doorbell echoes through the house and into the back yard through some of the open windows. With a quick glance to one another again, we make our way inside. If we wanted to catch any of the conversation taking place, we had to be within ear shot and we knew if any uniformed people showed up at the house, it obviously was a conversation about us.

Quietly, we slip in through the sliding door which leads us straight into the kitchen. Holding our breath, we strain to hear the conversation coming from the front door but, not to our surprise, we could barely hear. Nodding my head slightly, we carefully slip into the living room and place ourselves directly behind the couch. This gives us the best spot to hear everything far clearer. It also keeps us out of sight, so the odds of getting caught eavesdropping is far less likely.

"I told you all before, I am not giving Alise and Jemma to you. Money means nothing when it is that or my girls." The irritation in her voice is clearly present as this had been the third soldier this week taking time out of their day to come to our home.

"Please, Lillian, hear me out." The floor creaked slightly by the door which lead me to believe he must have shifted his weight as he spoke. I could tell already I did not like him, no matter who he was or what he might look like.

After a brief pause, the squeaky hinges on the door gave away the fact she had opened the door more. "Alright, James, I will listen to what you have to say but only because you were Aaron's favorite recruit. You were like a son to him, you know."

"Yes, I know. Why else do you think I am the one here trying to convince you to let me protect the girls?" He removed his hat revealing his dark brown hair, and slowly entered the house.

The door closed followed by footsteps as they made their way into the living room, the couch sighed slightly as James awkwardly sat down on it, holding his hat tightly in hand. Alise looks over at me as her breathing begins to increase, I place a finger over my lips as I attempt to tell her to stay quiet or she will give up our hiding place. I could hear our mother ask this soldier something, followed by steps leaving the living room only to return from the kitchen a few moments later. She must have gotten James something to drink, because you could hear the ice hit the side of the glass slightly as he took a sip. A creak came from the rocking chair on the other side of the living room as she sat in her favorite chair.

James clears his throat as he places his half empty glass on the side table and stands. The floor creaks as he walks over to the fireplace where he stands and admires the pictures sitting on the mantel. Aaron had a small version of one of the photos in his wallet, worn and slightly faded. But that had never stopped him from pulling the photo out and showing anyone and everyone who would let him.

"Why are you really here, James?" She broke the silence while her dark green eyes focused on him suspiciously as he admired the family photos.

He turns and looks to her shifting his weight from one leg to the other slightly. "When Aaron was shot on our tour to Europe, he made me promise to look after you and the girls. He said he knew I was young, but I could help protect all of you. I don't want to be the one to alarm you but something big is coming, Lillian, and, unless you trust me, I will never be able to keep the promise I made to Aaron." He returns to the couch and sits down looking to her with a serious facial expression.

"I am not sure if Aaron told you or not, James, but I do not need protection from you or the army." She crosses her arms as she glares at him. "What exactly do you mean when you say something big is coming? Whatever it is, I can handle it, and I can protect my daughters all on my own."

He let out a loud sigh as he rubs his temples. "I honestly don't know the full extent of what is coming, but what I do know is there is talk that this war is about to go nuclear. The only way I know how to keep all of you safe is for you and the girls to come with us to the bunker up at Fort Exodus."

She let out a slight laugh. "I am not going anywhere with the army, James, and I will be damned if you even think of taking my girls." Her look turned fierce as she was growing tired of this conversation. Aaron had known she was strong. Why would he ever think it was a good idea to have this child take not only her but Jemma and Alise to Fort Exodus? It made no sense.

"Lillian, stop being irrational and actually use the brain we all know you have. You know the war will eventually turn to this. The question is not if, but when. You and I both know those girls are special, would you really let them die because of your stubbornness?"

I glare through the couch at where James' back should be, he sounds far too young to be telling our mother what she can and can't do. He may have known our father, but he did not know us or what any of us are capable of.

"I will not give you or the army my daughters. I know damn well they would be used to create those super soldiers. Aaron told me all about what goes on in Fort Exodus." Quickly, she jumps up out of the rocker, her voice raised even louder as she moved towards the door.

"Lillian, you are going mad. Even if super soldiers existed, which they don't I might add, Aaron knew if he told you anything, it would break protocol. I believe in the time I got to know him, I learned enough to know he would never have jeopardized his career and your safety."

During all of the screaming between James and Mother, Alise had begun to cry. I held her tightly to me as we sat and listened to the conversation which was growing more and more heated by the second. It took a moment for us to notice James had gotten off the couch and they had moved the conversation back to the front door.

We strained to hear the muffled voices and quietly peek out the front window to see James get back into the SUV. It backed out of the driveway and drove away. Sobs seemed to be coming from our mother as she closed the front door. Alise wanted to do nothing more than go over to her and soothe her but I, again, had to stop her or Mother would have known we had been listening in on the conversation this whole time. Nudging Alise towards the kitchen, we slowly go back outside and over to the tree once more. As we reach the tree, Alise begins to cry heavily.

"She wouldn't send us with that soldier, would she?" Alise looks to me for the answer, her one green and one blue eye focused on my face. I knew there was always a possibility our mother might not have as much of a choice as she thinks she does when it involves the army, but I knew the answer that at this time Alise needed to hear most.

"Of course she won't. Don't be silly." I held my head up high as I did what I always do for her, protect her by ignoring the fear I feel creeping up inside of myself. To show my sincerity, I carefully remove a leaf that is stuck in her long dark brown hair.

"Girls!" Hearing our mother's voice draws us back to reality as we turn to see her standing in the door, beckoning for us to come inside.

Alise gives me a terrified look as a fresh set of tears begin to well up in her eyes. I place a hand on her shoulder, offering her a soft reassuring smile, before leading her back to the house. As we enter, Mother is sitting at the table sipping some freshly brewed coffee. Her dark auburn hair is tied up in a tight bun on top of her head, which she often did when she was trying to solve something that seemed to be just out of her grasp. When she sees us, she motions towards the two seats on either side of her. We hesitate for a moment before sitting at the seats she had gestured to.

"Your father's old training recruit, James, was here. He has invited us all to go stay with him at the base where he works for a short time." She looks between us. "We decided he will be coming back here in a few hours to take us there, which should give us all plenty of time to pack. What I need from both of you right now is go up to your rooms and pack a few things you cannot live without, as well as some clothing. I do not know how long we will be there but I want you to have a couple changes of clothing just in case."

"We are all going?" Alise questions as she emphasized the word "we" while looking into our mother's eyes.

"We will talk more about this after you go get ready. Please, no more questions for now. Go to your rooms and pack. Quickly now, James will be back in a little while." She waved her hands at us and sent us to our rooms to get ready.

Without uttering another word, Alise and I walk up the stairs and over to our rooms which are across the hall from one another. Understanding the hurry we were truly in, it took me not much time to pack at all. Alise though, seemed to be spending more time crying than packing, her crying drifted out of her room through the small hallway and into my room. Her cries made it difficult to concentrate on what all I wanted to take with me but, in a way, I did understand why she was upset. I was too, or at least I thought I was. This whole situation had gone through my mind quite a few times these past few weeks, I had imagined situations where the army burst through the door and picked us up out of our beds while we were sleeping. The fact this was the outcome I had not prepared for made it a lot less stressful.

Content with what I picked to take with me, I joined Alise in her room to help her, she had still not made it past grabbing her backpack. I walk quickly over to her dresser, open the drawer and pull out a few sets of clothing before putting them into her backpack. As I turn to grab some socks and other items, the doorbell rings, which sends Alise into another large crying fit.

Blinking, I grabbed her favorite stuffed teddy bear which was on her bed and hand it to her. I add the last few things to her backpack while she sits on the floor watching me. I point to the backpack, which she picks up slowly. I go to my room and pick up mine and place it on my shoulder. I look around my room for a few moments before picking up my favorite stuffed husky. I knew I was far too mature for things like stuffed animals but for some reason it still comforted me. Holding it tightly to my chest with one hand, I use the other to hold Alise's hand and we both walk down the stairs.

At the bottom of the steps, Mother had already opened the door revealing James who has two armed soldiers on either side of him who looked twice his age. This was my first real glance at him, besides that first moment when he exited the SUV which had left much to the imagination. I had imagined he had a cruel hateful, ugly appearance to him, but the reality was he was quite handsome and his kindness showed as he turned his attention to us.

 He smiles up at us as we take the steps one at a time, which I believed was due to Alise trying to lengthen the time it would take for us to have to leave. When we finally reach the bottom step, James motions for one of the soldiers to take our backpacks to the SUV. He then moves slightly out of the way so we can walk out the front door.

As we are about to go outside Alise stops cold in her tracks and turns to our mother. "Mommy? Where is your suitcase?" She may have not always been the sharpest but she did seem to take notice of small things, like a missing suitcase, a lot quicker than I ever did.

"I have a few things to do here first before I can join you. Don't you fret, my dear, I will be right behind you." She smiles at Alise before turning her attention to me. "Jemma, please take care of your sister for me."

I nod slowly. "I will."

"Good girl." She kisses both of our foreheads and sends us on our way to the SUV where the soldiers hold our backpacks. As we walk down the sidewalk to the truck, one of the soldiers closes the trunk after placing the backpacks into it.

"Lillian, someday you will see this is all for the best." James spoke in a gentle whisper as he watches us walking away from the house.

The time it took to go from the house, down the path, and to the SUV felt longer than it should have. Time had almost completely stopped as it felt like all was moving in slow motion.

"I will catch up with you both very soon." She waves to us as she smiles her reassuring smile, her voice drawing us back to reality once more.

I take a deep breath before climbing up into the back seat without much thought to it. I look around at the black leather seats, and how another soldier is sitting silently in the driver's seat waiting patiently for us. Content enough in the SUV, I turn to Alise and hold out my hand to help her in. She is crying again, and her words are inaudible as she begins to cry harder.

"Come on, Alise." I try speaking soothingly to her as I usually do to get her to focus on the task at hand as well as to calm her down.

"I can't, Jemma. I can't go without Mom." She looks up at me, tears staining her bright red cheeks.

"You have to, Alise." I make a firm facial expression, hoping she would take me a bit more serious. "Please." I look from her to our mother and James then to the two soldiers who are watching us.

Alise shakes her head, quickly turns and runs back over towards the house. As she runs as fast as she can, the soldiers who are standing close by the SUV snap into action and chase after her. They didn't make it to her before she reached our mother though, she even slipped past James as he tried to grab her. The guards and James stopped suddenly in their tracks during all of this as something catches their attention. To everyone's surprise, the unforeseen danger we were all being warned about is upon us.

Sirens begin to blare loudly, we all turn to the south to see that someone dropped an atom bomb 50 miles away from us right on downtown Denver. As it hits its target, the ground begins to shake, a mushroom cloud erupts quickly into the sky.

CHAPTER 2

I scream loudly to my sister and mother as I begin to feel the ground shake, rocking the SUV. I look out the back window of the vehicle and see a large mushroom cloud rising quickly over Denver. What was that thing they taught us in school about mushroom clouds? Before I could think about it too much more, I make an attempt to exit the SUV, only to be blocked by the soldiers as they quickly take their places on either side of me, which gave me no way to exit the vehicle. James jumps quickly into the front seat and yells to the driver. "Forget them, we have to go now!"

You could easily see the aftershock wave that was quickly making its way towards us. The driver without question put his foot straight to the floor causing the vehicle to screech as it makes a tight U-turn out of our driveway and speeding north, taking me away from not only my home, but my family, and my town.

As we speed away, I continue to stare out the back window as my mother and sister grow exceedingly smaller, I let out a loud gasp as the aftershock wave hits the house and, with one swift movement, the whole area is consumed by it, leaving destruction in its wake.

"No!" I call as I reach my hand towards where my house was consumed by the wave. I slowly turn in my seat and stare silently ahead without any other words.

The ride north was silent. How we managed to remain ahead of the aftershock, I would never understand. It almost seemed supernatural. The tension coming from the two guards beside me helped inform me I was not the only one feeling anxious about what had just happened in Denver. The road went on for days, and it felt like we had been on it for hours. Even though there had been so many reasons to cry about what all happened this day, not once had I shed a tear, even though I felt like I should have. After all the feelings I should have been able to acknowledge, I felt nothing. I had gone numb.

As the sun slowly set, we made it to the bunker where James and the rest of the army had their base. I could feel the soldiers relax slightly beside me as it came into view. The whole compound is surrounded by a chain link fence to keep people from coming or going without permission.

The guard on post searched the SUV with his flashlight and muttered something into his walkie talkie, once he gets a response he nods to the driver and lifts the bar blocking the entrance. We drive into what appears to be a parking garage. Barricades were up to prevent people from traveling up to the higher levels, which forces everyone in only one direction. Down.

At the bottom of the parking garage, two more guards stand at a door, waiting for us. In between them stands a large man with a very irritated look on his face and his arms crossed as he stares down the SUV.

James turns to me offering a slight smile. "Welcome to Fort Exodus. Once we stop, I will show you to your living quarters. The bunker is large but, given some time, it will become easier to navigate. It will be like you have lived here your whole life. I do ask two things of you though, do not wonder outside the fort. After what we saw in Denver today, I hope you understand why leaving is a bad idea. We have no way of knowing if and when they will strike again, and the radiation can and will kill you if you are not careful. The second thing is please do not disturb the guards. They are here to protect us all, they do not need any form of distraction. If you need anything, I will be there to help as best as I can, especially since I have been assigned to watch over you while you are here."

I blink at him showing I heard what he said, but whether I would stick to his rules, that was for me to decide later on. I still did not like him, and taking me from my family whom may or may not still be alive, felt unforgivable.

Once the SUV parks by the door, the soldier to my left exits and offers me his hand to help me get out of the vehicle. James had already gotten out and was talking to the bigger man in full gear. As I get closer I can hear what they are saying much clearer.

"You were ordered to bring all of them, James." The man glares at James as he shook his head in irritation.

"We had complications, Lieutenant." As the Lieutenant is about to question what sort of complications could keep him from a direct order, he adds, "Someone dropped a bomb on Denver. We were lucky enough to get out of the radius of the aftershock in time. With that surprise, it did not exactly give us time to grab any of the others."

The Lieutenant sighed as he set his dark brown eyes on me, and motions for me to come closer. I look to James who nods his head. I hold my head up high and walk over to them. The Lieutenant circles around me with his hands now behind his back before he looks into my eyes. He pauses. "How strange, she has two different colored eyes." He lifts my chin to get a better look at my eyes in the light.

"Her and her sister both have heterochromia. It is rare but not as rare as one might think."

"Fascinating, but you and I both know there is much more to the heterochromia eyes than just that. Please take her to the infirmary for a physical." With that he begins to walk away only to stop and look back at James. "Oh, and James, please bring me the results of her tests right away once you get them. You had better hope you got the right sister."

"Yes, sir. Follow me, Jemma." A guard at the door opens it and we both walk inside.

We walk through what appears to be a long hallway. As we pass, people stop and stare for a moment before whispering amongst themselves. I dislike all this attention so I decide to turn my attention to the walls. I notice every wall has a sign painted with arrows to show which direction to go to get to specific locations. Such as the infirmary, or the cafeteria.

James takes me first to a long corridor where all the rooms are. He stops us in front of the room numbered 101B. Using a key card, he swipes over the corresponding key pad and the door quickly whooshes open. The room is far bigger than I had expected. It has a bed, desk, dresser and even a small bathroom with a shower. "This is your room. My men will have your things brought here by the time you get back from the infirmary." James handed me the key card for my room before adding. "You can leave that here if you want, no one will take it."

Blinking, I look down only to now realize I still had my stuffed husky, which I was holding tightly. I nod reluctantly, entering my room and place it on my bed by the pillow.

"Come along." James spoke with a slight chill to his voice as he leads me back out of my room. Once outside the room, the door closes and locks automatically behind us. We continue back up the hallway the way we came, following the signs that lead us to the infirmary.

The door opens to the infirmary revealing a small room, with a surgical table which has a tool tray resting beside it, a few feet away is a desk where the doctor is sitting. She looks up as the door opens. "Ah, James! Lieutenant Grey said you would be stopping by today. Is this the girl?" The doctor is a slender grey-haired woman who, in my opinion, wore her hair up in what looked like too tight of a bun. "Please do come in, I do not bite." She gave a grin as I looked up at James to see he was smiling even though the joke was not funny at all.

I enter slowly, James follows behind me. Even if she did bite, that did not scare me, it was all the pointy tools that rested so comfortably on the tool tray that scared me. She looked me over, took my blood pressure, my weight, and checked my nose and throat before admiring my eyes. As a last set of punishment, she took some of my blood before letting us leave the infirmary, promising me that if I need anything to not hesitate to ask. That was not going to happen, but I gave a fake smile and wave as we exit the room.

As we are about to leave the infirmary, James turns and asks for the results as soon as possible. The faint sound of sirens play over the intercom as we walk up the hall. Soldiers rush past us and James looks to me with a bit of fear to his facial expression. "You can find your way back to your room, right? I have to go." He rushed off before even hearing my answer.

I guess I will have to find my own way around. I sigh as I look around and try to get my bearings back. I walk through a few hallways until I find a sign that tells me where to go, and I walk quietly back to my room as more soldiers and people rush past me in both directions. When I finally do find my room, I open the door and scan it slowly, spotting my backpack sitting directly in front of my bed. I walk over to it and, for a few minutes, I put my clothing in a dresser, pretending this place would ever give me the satisfaction of feeling at home. Sighing, I sit on the bed and pull the husky up to my chest and close my eyes.

At thirteen years old, not only was I taken away from my family, but I have no way of knowing if any of them are even still alive. The only fact I know is the aftershock wave that hit is a cloud of destruction and if anything survived, it would be a miracle. I could not see any of what the cloud had done, therefore, that still meant there was a chance everything was fine. Even with the odds stacked against them, I had to believe they were still out there, still alive. If that was the only thing I had left to hold onto, it was the only thing still holding me back from the darkness which would eventually find me.

 I can hear what sounds like drums as the whole fort shakes. I lay on the bed and stare up at the light as it rattles and sways wildly around. It did not take me long before I fell asleep to the drumming in my head. I was not sure what the sound was but I had a feeling it was not drums at all, but possibly bombs that had lulled me to sleep that first night in Fort Exodus.

CHAPTER 3

During the night a total of over one hundred bombs fell throughout all of the United States, most aimed to hit as many major cities as possible, but some strayed and hit little towns as well. The bombs left nothing but devastation everywhere they fell, and radiation that would take years to be safe for anyone again.

The people of Fort Exodus spoke in silent whispers about how they had heard guards and soldiers claiming that outside the walls of the fort it was no longer safe, as well as the radiation levels were worse than ever. Which meant there was a very good chance that unless the levels went down, no one would ever be allowed to leave Fort Exodus. The guards who were required to go out, now were required to wear hazmat suits and have Geiger counters on them at all times. If radiation was too high, they were required to be quarantined inside Fort Exodus with the rest of us until it is safe once more.

The days seemed to go on forever. With no windows this deep, underground time was becoming more difficult to grasp. As well as what day it was. There was a routine though which helped everything seem a little more normal. Every morning around what I would guess as 8:00AM, the lights turned on automatically, notifying everyone who was not already awake, that it was time to get up. At noon a bell sounds in all rooms to indicate it was time for lunch and by 9:00PM a slight flicker of the lights indicates you have a total of five minutes to get to your room or risk having to find it in utter darkness.

I spent most of my first week in Fort Exodus wondering the different hallways, purposely getting myself lost so I could find my way back to my room. I even attempted it a few times blindfolded, on the off chance I found myself out in the hall at 9:05. It would have been a more successful experiment, had people and walls not been in the way most of the time.

James set me up to join the school in the mornings the following week, after everything had begun to settle down. Everyone was returning to school now, and it was a good time to go ahead and send me as well. That way he did not have to keep an eye on me at all times. He claimed he had other things to do besides babysit me. Which could have annoyed me, but I didn't want him babysitting me either. At thirteen, I did not need a babysitter, I could take care of myself.

In the evenings after dinner, I had to go see the doctor for more tests, which they just called checkups. But I knew better. The tests were as simple as walking on a treadmill to swimming a lap in a pool, or answering questions about what I thought an oddly misshapen ink blot looked like. Sometimes for entertainment, I would say the shape looked like something extravagant and intricate just to see what sort of reaction they would have. On some occasions they would get confused, which caused them to study the ink blot, sometimes for a long time while they try to figure out how it got such an intense response from me. Other times they would shake their heads, completely amazed at how much I had grown in such a short time.

"I know what you are doing, Jemma." James stares blankly ahead of us as he walks me back to my bedroom.

"What am I doing exactly?" I turn to look up at him curiously. I can see the disapproval on his face which would almost make me feel bad if it actually mattered. Which it didn't. I was not here to seek his approval. I am here because I didn't have a choice.

"You are a smart girl. Why can't you take all of this seriously?" He sighs as he turns to look at me with his fierce dark green eyes.

"I am so tired of going to these 'sessions' with the doctor. Why am I not allowed to spend time with the kids my own age? I go to class with them every day and yet I don't know a single one of them." I look at him seriously. "Do you know how it feels to be an outcast? They all look at me like I am some sort of freak."

"You can get to know them better in your classes."

"That's not the same. They don't want to talk to me and every time I try to hold a conversation with them, they walk away."

James let out a sigh. "Fine. You can spend some time with some of the kids your age at the training sessions you will be joining. Hopefully, that will keep you from complaining as much."

"Thank you!" I exclaim with excitement before I pause and blink at him. "Wait, what sort of training?"

"The doctor said you should be just fine starting training with some of the other children now."

"You are making no sense. What sort of training?" I raise a brow at him as I eye him curiously. How could I have seriously not seen this coming?

"You will see." James points to my door which I unlock before stepping inside.

"That still does not explain anything." I manage as the door slowly closes between James and myself. I did catch a clever smile come on his face as he turns and walks away. Huffing, slightly irritated, I walk over to my bed and sit down. The way he had left me in suspense felt more of an annoyance then staring at a spot of ink that was supposed to be of some sort of significance, like an animal or some other shape. To me it looked like an ink spot, but what do I know? Laying down, I stare up at the roof, pondering what sort of training I was about to be put through. At exactly 9:05 the lights go out and I am already fast asleep, dreaming about what sort of day tomorrow might bring.

Training turns out to be a hundred times worse than looking at ink blots. There are a total of maybe ten kids, including myself. They all look like they are misfit rebels who don't belong, all angry and as out of place as I am. What caught me off guard the most though about this little band of rebels, is that I had never once seen any of these kids in my school class. Even though they all looked angry all of the time, in their own way they seemed far more accepting than those in school.

The trainer, however, is a cruel tall woman whose hair is tied up in a tight bun on top of her head, and the balding spot near the front lead me to believe she has used that hairstyle for far too long. She also has a unibrow that reminds me of a large hairy caterpillar crawling across her face as she lectures us. She is cruel and constantly ridiculing everything we do as though we would never be good enough or do well enough, no matter how many times she yells at us.

"This cannot be legal!" I raise my voice causing all nine of the other kids and the trainer to stare at me, moments after I had been hit square in the face by a total of five tennis balls. My face burned and I could smell the blood that was beginning to come from my lip and nose.

"Legal has nothing to do with this." She walks over to me holding one of the balls that had hit me in the nose, I could even see a little bit of my blood on it. "In the outside world, do you really think someone will care about what is and is not 'legal'?"

"No, they won't."

"Exactly, we are not doing this training as a punishment. We are doing this because, when it is safe again to go outside, you need to be prepared for anything. Legality has been thrown out the window at this point, children. The moment the bombs fell, the rules changed. It is eat or be eaten, kill or be killed. Just because you are children, does not mean anyone will be less likely to kill you. If you even look like a threat, you will die. It is how the world is now, and you need to understand that. I know all of you think I am a terrible person but what you don't know is that I want you to survive out there. If being a horrible person keeps you alive, then it is worth it." Her words sink in as we all look at her. We understood it could be bad out there, but it was not until this point that it really sunk in about how bad it truly was.

~ ~ ~

Between school and training, time began to pass a lot quicker. Birthday after birthday passed in what felt like the blink of an eye, there had even been times where I had not realized until a week later I even had a birthday. I lost all interest in getting to know any of the kids my own age. With all my training, I had no time. I did however decide it was in my best interest to occasionally find time every few days to irritate James, and purposely ignore some of the rules he had originally set for me.

On one such occasion when I was around 17, I recall casually walking over to the door that just so happened to be the main entrance and spotted a lone guard clearly doing his job at keeping people from leaving. I walk over to him and, with a soft smile on my face, I look up at him. "Well, hello there, handsome." The guard stands still and pretends I am not there, which obviously is possible since he towers over me, looking past me, as though I am not there at all. "I have noticed you here for the past few days. Do they ever let you leave? I see the dark circles under your eyes, are they feeding you well? Are they letting you sleep? You look exhausted." His face seemed to twitch slightly as he fights rolling his eyes at me. "James looks the same way honestly. I don't think they let him sleep at all. He is always so cranky. Is he cranky around you as well?" I turn and scan the hallway as I try and think of something else to talk about. "Do you think you could be a nice guard and let me go outside? I promise, I won't try to escape, again. We don't even have to tell that stuck up boss of yours, it could be our little secret." The guard seemed to be struggling really hard to continue to ignore me, as he tenses up to block the door even more. "Well, you cannot blame a girl for trying. Look, if you change your mind, I will be back tomorrow." I smile up at him and happily turn and begin to walk away. "Don't forget to ask for some food and sleep once in a while. Wouldn't want you to fall asleep at your post." I almost wanted to feel bad since, if it had not been for him actually falling asleep at his post one time, some of my classmates would not have gotten out and almost escaped once. Even so, I knew if anyone was going to get a lecture, it was me.

Unsurprised, I see James waiting for me by my room, his face a deep red as he glares at me furiously. The older I get the more he almost looked handsome when he was angry, the way his dark green eyes looked straight into my soul. It almost makes me wonder what they would look like when he isn't angry. It is a shame though that he is such a pain in the ass. "I told you not to talk to or distract the guards."

"He looked lonely, not to mention he is by that door all the time. He really needs to eat something and get some rest. He is beginning to look sickly, I am slightly worried about him." As I look up at James, I can see his right eye twitch slightly.

"He is doing his job, Jemma. He is eating and sleeping just fine." He wants to yell at me, I can feel it, but instead he runs a hand through his dark brown hair and sighs. "Don't do it again." He sighs again and walks away shaking his head while mumbling to himself.

I gave him a slight wave before slipping into my room. He looked exhausted. It could not be completely true that the other guard was sleeping just fine, perhaps all the events which had taken place over the past few years had caused some sort of insomnia for some of the soldiers, including James. I will never ask about it, mostly because I knew I would probably get yelled at for even bringing it up. But it made me wonder what this war was doing not just to the people here but the ones protecting us as well.

~ ~ ~

I only ended up finding one friend who felt like more of a sister to me than anything. She also attends the same training classes as I do. Her name is Bexie. She bore witness to one of my first interactions with James in Fort Exodus, and it was because of that interaction, we became instant friends. I had just been hauled back inside the base after having failed my first attempted escape, dirt caked all over my hair and hands and James as red-faced as ever. Once James was finished yelling and left me in my room for the night, Bex somehow picked my door's lock and snuck in to see me. We bonded instantly, as she tells me the story about how a few weeks prior, she and a few of our training group too had attempted to escape Fort Exodus with little luck. Claiming one of the guards had fallen asleep by the front door, they tried to seize the opportunity to escape.

Bex is one of the tallest in our training class, with long jet-black hair she always keeps down even when training. She also has one bright green eye and one dark brown eye. They always have some sort of mischief hidden behind them and a smile that always backs them up.

I had not noticed until it was pointed out to me by Bex that everyone in the training class has heterochromia, different forms of it, but heterochromia none the less. The kids in my regular classes, however, did not. I don't understand what makes a difference between the two groups, or why we are forced to train while those other children don't. It does not make sense. All I do know is one way or another there is some sort of significance as to why we are set apart. It was not long after this discovery though that I was removed from my school class all together to fully be submerged into training. I did not ask questions because it did not seem significant at the time, plus, with how busy I had been, it felt nice to only have one thing to focus on for once.

On my twentieth birthday, Bex comes bursting into my room with a large grin on her face, which, from quite a few personal experiences, was not going to end well. She was up to something. "What did you do now, Bex?" I grin at her as I wait to hear what chaos she had decided to create this time.

"It is not what I did, Jemma. It is what we are about to do." She smiles as she casually sits on the desk chair and faces me.

"I do believe the last time you said that, we managed to put the whole bunker into lockdown." I smirk as a flashback of my fifteenth birthday comes back to me as if it had been just yesterday.

Bex, somehow managing to find some "candles" in one of the many, many locked rooms no one but authorized personnel were allowed into, decided it would be a good idea to light them in my bedroom. Lucky for us though, we noticed pretty quickly they were in fact not candles at all, but dynamite. Thinking quickly, we ran the "candles" to the laundry shoot which was rarely used anyways, since everyone in base had to wash their own clothing. Which meant, once a week we had to go into the basement and do the laundry. Luck was in our favor since no one was actually doing laundry that day, or it could have turned out far worse than it did. We quickly tossed the dynamite into the shoot and watched as it dropped down a few feet before exploding.

It took two weeks to repair and clean up the mess we had made in the basement of the fort, not to mention the trauma we inflicted on the residents of Fort Exodus. We were not allowed to see each other again until Bex went under investigation, where they interrogated her until she told them where she had found the dynamite in the first place. Once the location was given, they relocated it to a new guarded spot, where she would not be able to find or get into again.

That was the longest two weeks of my life. I had no one to talk to, as well as receiving looks and whispers from the residents, saying things like "that is one of the girls who tried to blow up Fort Exodus." We did not try to blow up Fort Exodus. We more so accidently put the laundry room out of commission for a little while, because we almost blew up Fort Exodus. Completely different.

"Hey, if they had in fact labeled the dynamite better in the first place, then maybe we wouldn't have done that. Not to mention, we were still kids at that point in time." Bex's laugh was contagious and I soon found myself laughing as well.

"We? I believe it was your idea in the first place." I fight to say through the laughter. As I calm, I look to her a bit more seriously now. "So, what sort of arson are you planning for us this year?"

"Arson?" Bex continues to laugh loudly. "What do you take me for, Jemma, some sort of pyromaniac? I have nothing like that planned this year at all."

"Then what is it?"

"You will see." Bex grins with the knowledge that I hate those three words, ever since James had first said them to me.

"You know I hate surprises," I groan as she quickly stands up and turns to look at me from the door.

"I know, that is why I do it. I will see you tonight." With a slight wave of her hand, she grins and takes off out of my room. I can hear her laughter as she walked down the hallway.

Rolling my eyes, I shake my head. It is hard to be mad at someone who has the kind of bubbly personality that always seems to cheer you up instantly. It has always been slightly annoying how cheerful having her as a friend makes me, but I wouldn't change it for the world.

~ ~ ~

A knock comes to the door at 9:00. I quickly open the door and Bex is grinning at me mischievously again.

"Are you ready for your surprise?"

"You do know what time it is right? We have 5 minutes before the whole base goes into complete darkness."

"Why else do you think I have these?" She waves a flashlight slightly at me before pointing it to the hall. "Let's go before we have to use these, the last thing we want right now is to get caught and these will give us up for sure."

"Where are we going?"

"You will see soon, now let's go. Stay quiet and, whatever you do, don't get caught." Bex leads the way down the hallway in a direction I have never taken before. Which feels strange, I thought I had adventured all of these hallways pretty thoroughly. I guess I was wrong.

Through one corridor after another we move swiftly, with the occasional ducking into rooms so the guards did not catch us out past curfew. When we finally reach a large steel door the lights go out, sending the whole base into complete darkness once more. Pushing the door open, she flips on the flashlight and whispers, "This way." Quickly, we move up the stairs until we reach the top, I lost track of how many floors we had climbed since there are no markers on any of the landings we reach.

At the top of the stairs there is another steel door which, to my surprise, has no guard. I walk over to open it when Bex stops me. "Close your eyes." She grins as she waits until I comply and cover my eyes with my hands.

"You have made me walk through multiple hallways, as well as up who knows how many flights of stairs and decide to after all this time have me cover my eyes?"

"Pretty much, yes." I couldn't see her face but I knew she was sporting a smug smile.

As the door opens with a creak, a cool breeze moves across my cheek, I let out a sigh as the fresh air hits me. Even though it was fresh air, it smelled far different from what I once remembered all those years ago. A time long ago when Alise and I would sit under the pine tree in our back yard for hours without a single care in the world.

Bex walks me a little ways out before stopping and places my hand on what feels like a rail of some kind, the cold metal felt rough to the touch. I can hear her as she steps back, she continues to smile brightly. "You can look now."

As I lower my hands I gasp as I look at the world and the sky outside the bunker. In all my years, my dreams were of this world I had been kept from, but not once had it ever appeared like this. The forest across from the bunker is all dead, no leaves in sight. The little bit of road I can see is pitted with holes, created over time from weather and lack of the care they needed to remain smooth. As I look down at the Fort Exodus parking lot, it looks like it has been partly reduced to rubble.

Even within this new world, as changed and dead as it is, it is still everything I could have ever dreamed of and even more. My eyes move from distant trees to the search lights that scanned the rust covered cars in the yard between the bunker and the fence. I smile as I look to the star streaked sky and the glowing moon still offering its welcoming light, like it always did all those years ago.

"Do you like it?" Bex follows my gaze to the sky.

"Yes, it is perfect. Thank you, Bex." The moon felt entrancing and my eyes did not want to leave it even for a second, on the off chance if I did, it would all disappear, and leave me with nothing but a dream.

"I found that stairwell was not well guarded a few months ago, and I knew if anyone would like to see where it lead, it would be you."

"I appreciate you thought of me when you found it, thank you." I pause as a thought suddenly comes to me. "How easy do you think it would be to leave here?" I question aloud as I turn my gaze back down to the many cars between us and the gate, it looks like there are quite a few places we could use as cover while slipping past the guards.

"I don't know, just getting up here is a chore in itself." Bex looks around slightly as she keeps an eye out for guards. "Jemma," she speaks in a softer tone as she turns her attention to me. "It has been seven years. We don't know what sort of creatures reside out there beyond that fence."

"I understand that, but I am willing to risk it all against whatever creatures may be hiding in this new world. I have to try and get out of here. If Alise and my mother are still alive, I know they will be out there somewhere and I have to find them."

Bex lets out a sigh as she begins to feel defeated. "Alright, if you are going to try and do this act of recklessness, I am coming with you. There is nothing you can say or do that will stop me. If we are doing this, we are doing this together, but first, before we go, we need supplies."

I nod as we walk back to the door of the bunker. We make our way down the stairs, the flashlight leading the way back to my room. Bex slips into my room after I unlock it and sits on my bed. She watches me as she holds the flashlight up towards the ceiling. I slowly watch the door close behind me automatically before I look at her. "How soon can we go?"

"I need a few days to find and get some supplies ready." She looks at me and sees I am ready to leave at this very moment if given the opportunity. "Two days, Jemma. Give me two days to get everything we need and, after that, we can go."

"Alright, two days. After that, I am going to go with or without you and the supplies." Bex gave me a slightly shocked facial expression. I could see she was upset that I would leave without her too. It wasn't the plan, but if after two days she didn't show up with the supplies, I would go alone.

~ ~ ~

The two days following our conversation felt never ending. On the second day, I kept packing and unpacking my stuff as I fought to decide what I should bring. I finally gave up and threw my backpack down on the floor by the door, content it was packed how it needed to be. A knock came to my door at 9:00pm exact. I quickly open the door and Bex slips in. She is holding a large backpack and drops it heavily on the ground which caused me to jump slightly.

"What is in that?" I walk over to move it, only to realize it is far heavier than it looks.

"Food, weapons, clothing, blankets." She shrugs as she lists the items with ease.

"Weapons?" I tilt my head with confusion.

"Do you not listen to the rumors floating around here from the guards? They are about these beasts that were created because of all of the nuclear waste that came from the bombs, some of them are dangerous, others not as much." She pulls out a booklet which looks hand made. "I also found this in one of the guard's rooms. It looks like someone was drawing pictures and naming the creatures in this new world."

"I figured they were just horror stories, told to scare children." I carefully take the book from her and flip through the pages, one horrific creature after another. I started wondering if leaving the safety of Fort Exodus was a good idea after all.

"Horror stories and legends are known to come from some small glimmer of truth, and I don't know about you, but I would rather be safe than sorry. I also found this for you. Figured you might like it." Bex pulls out a long sword and hands it to me. "Since you preferred hand to hand combat. You should also take some of the food and blankets, on the off chance we get separated. I also recommend you take at least one gun, just in case."

"Thank you." I attach the sword to my backpack and transfer some blankets, food, and the book into my backpack before throwing it over my shoulder. Reluctantly, I take a small gun that happened to be on a gun belt and attached it to my waist, before throwing some ammunition into one of my backpack's pockets that was easy enough to reach. I would not use this horrifying weapon unless I absolutely had to. I am no fan of guns and knew I would always go for the sword first if given a choice.

Bex quickly organized which weapon she wanted for a worst-case scenario, as I grab my stuffed husky which was still sitting on the bed. Jamming it furiously into the side of my already overstuffed back pack I feel like I have everything I need now. I turn to Bex who is watching me curiously.

"Are you ready?" She questions as she hikes up the not as heavy backpack onto her back.

"I am ready." As the words escape my mouth all of the lights in the base turn off, submerging us into utter darkness once more.

CHAPTER 4

The air feels cold on my skin as we carefully slip through the door that leads us out onto the roof, where days prior I saw the moon for the first time in years. We begin to make our way down the damaged path towards the main level, spotting only a few guards on the way who are leaning against the wall which barricades the path. This tells us we have reached the ground level. The guards are busy talking to each other with their backs turned to the wall, which makes it almost too easy to slip past them. We crouch behind a van in the yard, the fence a few feet away in clear view from where we wait for the spot light to drift over our heads.

Bex leads the way, commenting quietly that she had gone back to the roof that same night she took me up there and found a simple escape route for us. Carefully, we dodge guards by hiding behind damaged cars, and we finally make it to the tall chain link fence. A bright flood light has been circling overhead for a while now, but we know once we reach the fence we are unprotected. As we watch it pass over us once more, we quickly race for the fence where she lifts some of it so I can slide under. We must not have timed it right, as the flood light fixated itself on us as sirens begin to blare, filling the once quiet night with ear shattering sound.

"Quickly, get under the fence!" Bex turns to look behind her at Fort Exodus as it erupts with soldiers coming into the yard. She quickly pulls the gate up a little more to give me a bit of extra room for me to go under.

I open my mouth to protest, but the sounds of dogs barking stopped my argument before I had a chance to even start it. I could see flashlights sweeping past vehicles as guards and soldiers exit Fort Exodus to stop us from leaving, they reminded me of ants rushing out of an ant hill.

"Go!" she shouts as she turns to me with a serious look on her face. "I will catch up, we did not go through all of this trouble for both of us to get caught. Find Alise and your mother, I will find you when I can. I promise."

Every sound around me echoes in my head as I quickly fall on my stomach and crawl under the fence after throwing my backpack through the hole. I turn to hold the fence up for Bex, only to realize she was no longer there. I get up quickly, pick up my backpack and run for the grove of dead trees across from Fort Exodus. I crouch behind a stump and begin to scan the yard for her, my heart pounding loudly in my ears.

The commotion of the escape brought out both James and Lieutenant Grey, both sporting the same concerned and irritated facial expressions.

"Find them!" Grey barks loudly at the scrambling soldiers. "When you do find them, bring them to me immediately!" He storms off furiously back into the fort.

"You heard him, bring them both back alive." James walks over to the fence and scans the trees. I almost thought he had seen me a few times as he stared directly at me but, to my surprise, he eventually turned away and went back to looking between the vehicles.

My heart races more, as it pounds loudly in my head. I scan the whole area frantically searching for Bex, hoping she will still be able to get out, wondering if she had found another way out and I had just missed it. I let out a slight gasp as I finally spot her. My heart races even more as she slips into the shadows by the fence. "Watch out!" I want to scream as she runs head first into James, who grabs her and pulls her into a rigid hold to keep her tightly in place, arms braced behind her no matter how hard she fights with him.

"I got one!" He yells as he makes his way back to the bunker.

"Let me go!" She thrashes furiously as she tries to get out of his alarmingly tight grasp.

"Grey wants you for interrogation and, if you know what is good for you, Bexie, you will tell him what he wants to know."

"Or what, James? You stopped me once, I will get out again." She snarls as she kicks at him which causes her dark hair to fall into her face.

"If you don't do what he says, there is a very large chance he will get that information from you by force."

"Force? You are off your rocker, soldier boy. Even if you have me, you will never get Jemma. She is probably long gone by now, and there is absolutely nothing you or any of your little buddies can do about it."

"We will see about that." James walks Bex to the door of the bunker and has a guard escort her back into Fort Exodus.

"I am not afraid of you or whatever 'force' you think you can put me through." Bex yells to James as she disappears behind the door.

I was so distracted by Bex I did not notice the guards who were now searching around the fence with a few of their dogs. Two dogs began to bark loudly as they stand in front of where I had slipped through. "She went under the fence!" one yells which causes James to rush over to where they are and quickly looks across into the trees once more.

"What do we do, sir?" The guard looks anxious as he turns first to the trees than to James.

"Leave her to the monsters, they will send her running back to the fort. She will be begging us to take her back by sunrise." James smirks slightly as he raises his voice slightly, knowing that I am still in ear shot. "I know you are out there, Jemma. You could make this easier on yourself and just come back now but, after years of having to keep an eye on you, I know better. So, if you survive the night and realize the big bad world is far worse than you think it is, we will be waiting for you." James turns to the guard as he lowers his voice. "Once the sun rises, begin searching the trees. Anyone who finds her will be guaranteed double rations for the next week. Make sure you bring her back alive, if the creatures don't get to her first."

The guards cheer as I blink and sink down behind the tree stump. If I stay, I could get the same fate as Bex, if not worse. But if I go, I could possibly find Alise and our mother. Bex's words fill my head as I contemplate what I want to do. *We did not go through all this trouble for both of us to get caught.* I decide I will leave, and come back for her once the bunker is not on high alert and after I find Alise. I wait until the guards begin to settle down. Once content it has calmed down enough that I can carefully move within the shadows of the trees, I make it past the fort.

As the night draws on, the moon's glow seems to be the only light available to help me see in this new world. As I walk, a curious flapping sound causes me to stop in my tracks and look around as I try to figure out where it is coming from. A large shadow comes over me and I look up, my jaw dropping instantly. High above my head in the sky a large bat flaps its wings while it looks directly at me. It is hard to tell for sure but it looks as though its wingspan is as long as a bus, its ears twitch before slightly pointing them towards me.

I always liked bats, especially the ones that remind you of a little fox with wings, and this large creature was kind of cute in an "I'm going to kill you" kind of way.

 I look around while I try to work out an idea of where I can run to escape getting killed by this monstrous creature, considering I have been out of Fort Exodus for only about five minutes, the last thing I need is to die before I even get more than a few feet from it. Knowing I can't stand here all night, especially with that gigantic bat hovering over my head just waiting for a pristine moment to swoop down and eat me alive, I have to come up with something quickly.

In the distance, I can see what looks like a small grocery store. I make a split second decision that place will be better than nothing. I take off running towards it. I can hear the bat as it flaps its wings and begins to follow me. The sound of this large beast only drives me to run faster towards the building, knowing I have to make it there as quickly as possible. I will not die here. I can't.

As I get closer to the grocery store, I notice the windows are all boarded up. I have to hope I have luck on my side as I run up to the door and try to open it. To my surprise, it opens at once. Slipping in as fast as possible I slam it shut behind me and lock it. Leaning against the door, I pant heavily waiting for my eyes to adjust to the darkness. I slowly move through the store blindly until my fingers fall on a flashlight, which, also lucky for me, turns on with no issue. I wonder the isles noticing the different cans of food as well as household items. I catch my reflection in the mirror and realize I will be making another stop on my way through town. I need an outfit that is not a bright green track suit given to me courtesy of the army in Fort Exodus.

I take a deep breath, taking out the sword Bex gave me as I venture deeper into the grocery store. I begin putting extra cans of food into my backpack, I only have a small amount of food given by her prior to our escape. I knew eventually I would need more, so I figured why not stock up now. I manage to find some medicine, which I put into one of the backpack pockets as well as band-aids. By the time I reach the back doors that lead to the storage area of the store, I believe I am completely alone. Which would have been another stroke of luck for me, if I had been right about it that is.

I slowly open the door to the back storage room and come to a complete halt. My flashlight gleams off something yellowy white a little ways off. As I move the flashlight slightly, I realize what the thing is attached to. A very large rat, and the yellow thing is its teeth. There are at least five of them, all eyeing me with big red eyes. If I could guess how large they are I would say about the size of a medium sized dog, with large spikes sticking up from their spines.

I shudder at the sight of them, which causes the rats to run straight towards me at a full sprint. I turn and run full force back through the door, slamming it hard into one of the rat's faces. I look for a lock but it seems to have been broken off long ago. My heart races as I stand in front of the door, holding it closed with all my might, waiting for them to overpower me and get through the door.

It does not take long for my fears to become reality. I swing my blade at the first one and connect immediately with its neck. The other rats fall back for a moment, shocked that one of their own is dead. Once the realization is over, it makes them furious. They all begin to rush and attack once again and, one after another, they all fall to the floor just like the first until there is none left.

I walk past the five motionless bodies lying in pools of their own blood and walk into the backroom. I'm confident if giant rats are the only issue I face in this new world, I will be set. Who am I kidding though? It certainly cannot be that easy.

In the backroom, I find a small office where I set up a sleeping bag on the floor. Once content with where I placed it, I take apart the desk and make a fire outside the office, using the desk and kindling and a few bricks to keep the fire from burning down the store while I sleep.

The glow makes the back room have an eerie look to it. I sit by the fire quietly. Watching the flames dance about, a feeling of comfort comes to me. I am safe at this moment and, after what all happened today, I am free from Fort Exodus' shadow. The army will spend the morning searching the trees, which I know will give me plenty of time to slip out of the grocery store and continue to make my way back towards my home.

A pang of guilt hits me as I think about Bex. After all she has done for me, I just left her there. The unfortunate knowledge that she will be guarded far more right now will make it impossible to go back. I'll stick to my decision to find Alise and our mother. Once I am with them again, we can work together to save her. I know they will help me. They are family and Bex is my friend. They will help her if I ask them.

I pull out the book Bex took with the different creatures in it and with a pencil I draw the large bat on one of the back pages as well as the rat creatures, leaving a name for them blank. I am not sure what I want to name them or if they should have a name. After I am finished drawing in the book, I put it aside. I can feel myself drift off to sleep, my mind sorting through the multiple scenario's that might unfold for me tomorrow, as well as the possible beasts I might meet. This leaves much stress on my mind as I drift off.

CHAPTER 5

The night feels like it went on forever. Being in a foreign location, every sound causes me to jump. It is likely just the old building settling but it is hard to say for sure. That was the one good thing about Fort Exodus, at least I was protected from creatures in there. My dreams were laced with images of the creatures I had seen from the book as well as the bat and rats I already had the pleasure of meeting.

Once I saw the sun shine through a slight gap in the boarded-up windows, I decide it is time to pack up and get going. Putting out the already dying fire, I pack up the few items I had taken out of my backpack and make my way for the front door.

As I open the door, the fresh cool air is welcoming. The rats had not smelled good before they died, but now that they have a chance to start to decay, they will only start to smell worse.

I scan everything around me and am facing a heavy shroud of fog which must have rolled in during the night. The fog gave an eerie feeling, but it also gave me comfort. It meant the soldiers from Fort Exodus would not be working very quickly in this, giving me a pristine opportunity to get some real distance while I know they will be preoccupied. Luck must still be on my side, I think to myself.

Looking up and down the street with nothing in sight, I put Fort Exodus behind me and walk my way down the street. Cars and trucks litter the streets, wheels missing and rust coating the once beautiful colored vehicles. As I walk past one, I look through the dust covered windows and see a skeleton. Its clothing tattered and its jaw wide open. I wonder if it hurt when they died. Did they suffer or was it instant and they felt nothing? I shiver slightly at the thoughts drifting around in my mind.

The closer to my hometown I get, the more I notice there are even more vehicles which seem to have been trying to leave Denver using this small town as an escape route. Bumper to bumper traffic make it difficult to cut through. Farther down, I can also see a pile up started with a single car running into a semi-truck. As I look upon the scene around me, I cannot help but feel the panic that must have taken place the day the bombs fell. I was out of the range of it and survived, but seeing all of this reminds me that many didn't get as lucky as I had that day.

Worry hits me as I recall Alise and our mother as the aftershock wave rushed towards us. Have I been naïve this whole time in assuming they were alive after all of this time? Especially after seeing all of this.

I sigh softly as I notice a gas station. My stomach seems to growl on cue reminding me that, after the events of last night, I have not eaten anything since dinner.

Entering the diner attached to the gas station, I notice it is one of the older styled diners. As I look around more, I wonder if they actually ate in the diner or if it was some sort of historical museum, considering the booth seats, jukebox, retro-styled floors as well as some records hanging on the walls. Walking over to the jukebox, I wipe the glass and peer inside at the records resting completely untouched. I could see a mechanism that would pick up and switch out records depending on what song the person wanted to listen to.

I wondered if it still worked but, having no way to check, I decide to leave it alone and sit down in one of the booths and eat something I stashed away in my backpack from the grocery store.

Borrowing one of the less dirty utensils which happened to be still wrapped up in a napkin on the table, I retrieve a can of pork and beans from my backpack. It is not until I have the can open and have already consumed three full scoops of the food that I realize how hungry I truly was.

As I am about to take another bite of food, I feel the hair on the back of my neck stand on end as I hear the sound of nails click against the floor. I feel like something is watching me, and its heavy breathing sends my heart racing once more. I hear it growl as I slowly place my hand on the hilt of the blade, preparing to fight yet another creature from this treacherous wasteland that I once called home.

I steady my breath as I tighten my grasp on the sword, in one swift movement I stand, spin around to face the vile creature and ready my sword for an attack. I raise my hands as I start to swing the sword, only to stop suddenly as I come face to face with a dog. Its brown eyes stare at me with confusion as it tilts its head before dropping a bowl from its mouth and placing it onto the ground. It nudges the bowl towards me with its nose. It is very wolf-like in appearance, yet it is tame. It pants as it tilts its head at me once more, curiously, before pawing at the bowl which turns my attention down to the empty bowl.

Raising a brow, I pick up the can of pork and beans from the table and pour some of its contents into the bowl.

It wags its tail at me as a sign of thanks and ate so quickly I wondered if it even tasted the food as it went down its throat. As I watch it eat, I wonder who it once belonged to and what ever happened to them, or if they are even still alive. I sigh at the thought and wonder why someone would leave their dog, especially one as gentle and kind as this one. I blink and notice the dog is gazing at me, licking its chops and wagging its long fluffy tail at me once more.

Losing interest in eating the rest of the food, I dump it into the bowl. I put the sword back in the sheath, pick up my stuff and make my way past the dog and slowly out of the diner. As I open the door to leave, a soft whimper comes from behind me. I turn to see the dog looking at me with a look of what could only be described as sadness and fear of being left alone.

I weigh my options as I stare at this dog's big brown eyes. "You're very good at that," I mumble as I walk back over to the dog and pick up its empty bowl, before going back to the door and opening it to leave. The dog stands still watching me, confused by what I had just done. I sigh as I roll my eyes. "Well? Come on then." It wags its tail as it walks past me, sticking its tongue out happily as it practically skips. I sigh and roll my eyes again while watching as the dog trots in front of me proudly. I decide to name him Kota, naming it after my stuffed husky I still carry with me even now.

As we make our way through the small town, I notice a clothing store. I walk over and fight with the door for a moment before it gives way. Flicking on the flashlight, relief comes the moment I realize no creatures are in here besides myself and the dog now named Kota.

I make my way over to the woman's department and wonder passed some of the mannequins. I shudder. Out of everything I have seen so far, those things were terrifying, even now. I pick out some black leather pants and a black top which has a corset style on the front of it. Smiling, I go over to the shoes and find a pair of boots before changing into my new outfit, tossing the ugly bright green jumpsuit into a far corner of the dressing room.

I peer into a dark mirror at my reflection. My long dark hair grazes past my shoulders all knotted up from lack of care. Even with the knotted up hair, this reflection I see feels more natural and, for once in my life, I feel like myself, the version of me I have always imagined I could be.

Smiling, I walk over to accessories and brush my hair before placing it up into a high ponytail, and putting the brush into my backpack. Content, I turn to Kota, shrug my backpack onto my shoulders and we head for the door. We walk past a mannequin wearing a black leather jacket. I stop and stare for a moment before taking it off of it and quickly slipping it into my backpack. I would attempt to remember this place. That way I could at least attempt to pay them back for the items I took. I had a feeling though they would not care one way or the other. If they were still alive, there were far more important things then a person coming into a permanently closed store and taking some of the clothing.

We make our way down the road towards my hometown, which felt even more like a ghost town than how the world already did. A place that once held so many memories for me, changed. Houses were in piles of rubble and there was evidence everywhere that people had looted many of the stores and homes, taking anything and everything they could carry.

I force back memories of this place, for fear they will fog the reality sitting in front of me. I stop at a sign tilted on an angle but I can read the name well enough. It has my hometown street on it. I can feel my stomach churn as I spot the driveway leading up to my house. I was home, but even so I have to understand there is still a very large chance the house I lived in could have been completely destroyed even if the structure still looks intact, just like so many other houses around here. I let out a deep sigh and begin to make my way down the road and closer to the house I was taken from seven years ago.

Chapter 6

The house I once knew from my childhood had been a grand plantation-style home, with white siding and burgundy shutters. The lawn was always in pristine condition with no weeds out of place, and in the back yard a large pine tree stood.

My father, Aaron, had the house built for my mother, Lillian, the year they got married. Sadly, shortly after the wedding took place the war had begun, and he was taken away to fight with the army once more.

Lillian always told him the home was too big for just her while he was away so, as a joint decision, they rented out the west wing to any military wives who were struggling during this tragic time.

Once Alise and I were born, the rental rooms slowly became more and more vacant. Only my mother's friend and coworker as well as her son had stayed in the grand plantation to help her with two young daughters, but in a few weeks' time, they too left us.

I took the time to look back on those memories because this house before me was not the place my father had built. This house before me had not only discolored siding but also had lost half of the siding on one side of the house. The windows were all broken and, if you looked closely, you could see all the curtains were torn and damaged. Some of the shudders remained on the house, but they only seemed to be attached by one nail tilting slightly to one side where they desperately hung. They will fall with the next big wind storm. It is inevitable.

The once kept grass now grew out of control. In some sections the grass was tall, impossible to even attempt to walk through. In other spots, it was all dead.

I walk to the side of the house and see the pine tree with some of its branches scattered around the trunk. I walk closer and the memory of Alise sitting under the tree with me the day I was taken away, drifts back. I felt happy that morning. If only I had known my life was about to change forever in an unexpected way.

I stand under the tree and look across the back yard and over to the door that leads into the kitchen. I carve my initials into the tree. If Alise is alive and looking for me, I want to make sure she knows I have been here. I run my fingers over the carved letters before putting the sword away and I make my way to the house.

The short walk from the tree to the house felt like it was over a mile long, as memories seemed to flood my mind even more, which causes my heart to pound loudly. The door to the house sits open slightly, either someone else had opened it and was in the house, or they had been there but already left prior to my arrival.

With a shaking hand, I open the door the rest of the way. It creaks loudly and echoes through the empty kitchen. The house feels cold and lifeless, and every room I enter, the furniture is either damaged or completely ruined. I begin to feel sorrow for everything I had taken for granted when I was here. Things you expected to last forever now show proof that that was not the case.

I spend hours looking in every room of the home, with little success in finding any proof anyone here had survived the bomb. I went through the living room and spot one of the pictures on the mantel above the fireplace. It was a picture of our father and mother. They were standing in front of a book case in the study. She was wearing a long lab coat, with her hair tied up in a bun, while he was standing proudly in his uniform. They had been celebrating something. They had champagne flutes as they cheer the photographer.

I scan the picture for a moment more, searching for anything it would tell me, and then, as if it jumps off the photo, I see it. On the ground by their feet, you can easily see a difference in texture on the carpet, as though something had been moved moments earlier.

Quickly, I rush to the study only to stop suddenly as I stare at books scattered everywhere as well as a secret room hidden behind a half moved bookshelf. I carefully move around the discarded books littering the ground and over to the slightly-opened bookshelf. With little effort, I move the bookcase to reveal the hidden room. In all the years we had been here, I had not once known about this room. But the real question was, did Alise?

As I enter the room, I notice it is almost the same size as our living room. I see the floor is littered with old newspaper clippings and as I scan the rest of the room, realize it is a lab. A set of surgical tables are placed on the far side of the room, shelves are full of jars with strange items in them, and in one corner of the room stands a skeleton. I stop and look at a few DICOMs on one of the walls behind the surgical tables and my heart begins to race once more. What was this room used for? Was something illegal going on here and no one knew about it?

Curiously, I pick up one of the newspaper articles littering the floor. It is one of the only ones that had been placed into a frame. I stare at the headline and feel anger creep up my spine as I shake uncontrollably.

Dr. Lillian McKnight Successful Cybernetic Experiment!

During the course of one year, Dr. McKnight's cybernetic experiment has finally proven that, with specific genetic manipulation, it is now possible to create something that can cure many, if not all, diseases in the world. By creating a human-like cybernetic that feels and is capable of making a connection with an ill human, McKnight claims this breakthrough will change all of modern medicine as we know it. McKnight also claims this success is now proven, all thanks to the use of her daughters.

The rest of the clip had been torn, leaving me with more questions than answers. If Alise and I were experiments mother had used, was that why she was arguing with James about not wanting him to take us? Was the real reason she didn't want him to take us because she did not want her "experiments" to fall into the army's hands? Fury exploded in me as I crumple the newspaper clipping and throw it to the ground.

I pull the picture of her and Father out of the frame and rip her out, throwing her side of the picture to the ground.

Not content with just doing that, I begin throwing everything on the shelves to the floor, they all smash the instant they make contact with the tile floor. I turn my attention to the chairs, throwing them and other less breakable objects at the DICOMs.

I leave the room completely destroyed. I know, as I completely destroy the lab, I will never return to this house of lies again. If Lillian is alive, I honestly don't even care anymore if I ever see her again.

What I do care about is if she is alive, Alise is with her, and I have to find her. Determination to find her grows even stronger. I now know I have to find her. If we were Lillian's experiment, there is a large chance Alise is still in danger. I will find her and convince her to leave with me or, if she is imprisoned, I will free her.

My only problem is Colorado is a big place to get lost in, especially when you do not want to be found. I have no idea where to start, but I have to start somewhere.

Chapter 7

Fear and anger fills me as I leave the house, determined to leave my past and all that I knew behind me, not knowing what part of my past was real and what wasn't anymore. I walk along the road thinking if I was Lillian, I would not have headed north in the same direction as Fort Exodus but south towards Denver, possibly even past Denver. I will make my way towards Denver, keeping clear of the highest radiated areas as I make my way around it. Then wherever the road leads me from there, hoping I will find someone who may have an idea where I can find Lillian, and my sister.

I lose track of time again and it is not until I hear whimpering behind me, I notice I am not alone. I look to the sky and towards the sun high up in it, which makes me think it has to be at least noon.

I search around and settle for a bench by an old tourist stop. Sitting down, I grab a can of food and the dog bowl. I pour half of the food in the dish before placing it on the ground and begin to eat my portion of the food. Kota slops up his food happily.

I scan the area around us and notice a large billboard showing a beautiful landscape as well as some mountains, claiming this picture is the Garden of the Gods and it is only a few miles south from here.

After we eat our fill, we continue our walk south. Knowing this place is only a few miles, it will be a good location to stop for the night before we continue our journey. Maybe, if we are lucky, we will find someone who can give me some answers.

A few miles turns out to be a down right lie; we have been walking for over an hour and a half. My muscles have begun to burn as I force myself forward, and only stop long enough to get a drink of water. Perhaps the mileage is referencing driving a vehicle, although I doubted any vehicles took this road anymore.

Iron Heart

Once we finally arrive, I notice The Garden of the Gods is not as breathtaking as the pictures had shown. The nuclear fallout took away some of the natural beauty it once had, but the one thing it could not touch was still there; the red rock formations which were standing tall and as proud as they ever have.

Trails lead deep through some brush and straight to a large red rock formation. Up ahead of us, I can see two large stones spelling out "Garden of the Gods," with overgrown grass covering the path that circles around it.

I hesitate as I spot a few large man-made shelters in a field not too far from the stone signs, the words of the trainer in Fort Exodus ring in my head. *The moment the bombs fell, the rules changed. It is eat or be eaten, kill or be killed.* I take a deep breath and move toward the shelters. I prepare for the worst-case scenario as I move closer. I make a quick note that there are at least five shelters obstructing the beauty of this park, which has now clearly been turned into a living area and a market. Fresh vegetables sit in boxes by shelters, which is proof that somehow food was still capable of being grown in even the worst of environments, so long as it was given the right kind of care.

A large woman spots us and leaves the group of people, walking over to welcome us. Her face beams one of the widest smiles I have ever seen in my life.

"Hello there! What brings you to the Garden of the Gods?" Her thick accent is not one common here in Colorado, and makes it slightly difficult to grasp as she speaks her words.

"I am just looking for a place to camp for the night."

"Ah, a traveler, are you? My family and I are too. We came down from Michigan, we did. Before the big boom and all." Her cheeks turn red while she cheerfully speaks of her family.

She is too happy in my opinion, it honestly feels painful to watch that much cheerfulness. With all of the destruction, it is completely unusual, absurd even. Perhaps she is ill.

"Do you have food? If not, we have plenty to go around. Say, you're not going to sleep over there, are you?"

She follows me around while I attempt to find a decent spot to set up my sleeping bag for the night. I turn to her, blinking slightly. "Is here a bad spot?" I look at her, wondering if this is a sign she doesn't want me in the camp after all.

"Well, if you don't mind your pooch there as well as yourself becoming something's dinner, it is a fine spot."

Kota whimpers up at me as he wags his tail slowly. "I suppose that would not be a good idea." I let out a slight sigh.

"Good, you will sleep in my shelter then. No arguing." She walks away but turns to look at me suddenly. "I am Maggie, by the way. It is nice to meet you both. What are your names?"

"I am Jemma, and this is Kota."

Maggie talks the whole way over to the crowd who she introduced us to, than talks more through dinner which, according to their rules, is abruptly an hour before dusk. This is followed by curfew at exactly dusk.

"Why such an early curfew?" I question as I watch the outside fires getting stoked.

"The night animals, of course. The ones in the day are not nearly as bad as the ones which like to show up in the night." The way she says this makes me wonder what sort of monsters she has come across. "We saw a bat fly off with some of the cattle the other night. Ever since, we do not stay out past dawn should we become the next ones to be carried off."

"Could you not find something to keep the bats from coming after your cattle?"

"Oh goodness, no!" Her voice is fearful as she turns her eyes to me. "Have you not seen one of those things? If they want it, they will find a way in no matter what you do to keep them from it."

Having seen one with my own eyes, I knew she was right. If it wanted one or more of the cattle, there was nothing anyone could do to stop it. As much as I hated to admit it, at least it was going after the cattle and not us.

Dusk comes quickly, sending everyone in camp into their shelters. Kota and I follow Maggie into hers where we continue our conversation we were having before. She mentions other animals to look out for. She tells me about a cougar with teeth so long, they go down past their chin. The description reminds me of the sabre-tooth tigers, from millions of years ago. She also warns me about the porcupines, the size of a small car with quills the size of swords and just as sharp, which they will use to attack anything they considered a threat.

I question her on if she has heard anything about a location where I might find a large group of scientists. To my luck, she mentions there is a place a little south of here where there are homes built into a mountain. The homes unused, just a front to where the location actually is. Beneath them.

The scientists call the place Genesis. It is a large compound deep down into the earth, where they conducted multiple different types of experiments. According to Maggie, these creatures which have taken over the world since the nuclear attack may have been released by Genesis. The story goes that Genesis was all set to release them into the world the moment the bombs fell. To create a new form of chaos for those who somehow managed not to die from the bombs.

If that all was true though, I wonder who dropped the bombs, and had it also somehow been part of the plan, like the release of all of the terrifying creatures in this new world? Or had the bombs dropping been a lucky accident, which they could use as a distraction and to become the blame for something far more sinister the scientists from Genesis created but had yet to release?

Sleeping felt impossible, thanks to the vivid conversation. I, for some reason, also was haunted by a dream that I was in Genesis and saw Alise being experimented on in one of the labs that looked identical as the one in the house. As the dream went on, I realized quickly it was not Alise who was being experimented on, it was me. Once that realization hit, I suddenly found myself on a surgical table, strapped in, unable to move. Scientists standing over me, ready to perform some sort of surgery while I was still wide awake, and no matter how hard I tried, I couldn't escape.

I wake from the dream in a cold sweat and, as I look around me, I realize the sun is not going to rise for a while. I hoped it was early enough that I could slip out before anyone could say goodbye.

I was shocked, as I am about to leave the shelter, and notice everyone running around and getting things done they could not complete during the night. Now that dawn had come, it was like the place took over where it had left off the night before. I can see people gathering eggs and others milking the cows that survived the night, I even saw some people peeling potatoes for breakfast.

Kota, who was by my side when I got up, rushes off to beg someone for a piece of food, clearly not caring what it was so long as it was edible.

I slowly scan the area where Kota disappeared to, I shrug and sigh loudly. Maggie invited me for food with them and then I told them that it was time for me to go. If Genesis is where they thought the scientists would be, that is where I had to go.

"Be careful out there now. There are many people just as terrifying as the beasts I warned you about last night. Oh, before I forget, if you do go south towards Genesis, be careful of the followers of the Glowing One. A couple of nut jobs, if you ask me."

Maggie gave me a small pistol for my travels, claiming it would be better to be safe than sorry. Unable to find any excuse to decline it, I took it without even one complaint. As I walk away from Maggie and her group, I thought about sticking around here a bit longer and helping them out. Even if that was something I desired to do, I knew my heart wouldn't be into it. I had to complete this mission first.

I had questions which needed answered, and I wasn't going to just sit back and wait.

Besides, I have to save Alise. I have no idea what sort of duress she is being put through, or if she is even still alive. But I have to try, even with the odds stacked against me.

I will eventually visit Maggie and her family again, once all of this is over and Alise is safe from our so-called mother at last.

Chapter 8

The sun shines bright above my head as Kota and I walk down the pothole infested roads and, for such a nice day, it is eerie that no birds ever seem to chirp any more. I was surprised I had not noticed this before. Perhaps they had no reason to sing anymore. I can't say I blame them.

I turn and look to the dead trees on the sides of the roads, and notice a murder of crows eyeing me down like if I stare back at them too long they will make me their next meal. Deep down I know being killed by a crow was next to impossible, considering they were scavengers and got their food from corpses, not live animals. But that did not change the fact that, if I disturbed them in any way, they will attack. I carefully watch them as they watch me continue down the road. With a deep breath I turn from them, confident enough to know they will not attack me.

Kota stops in his tracks and growls, his tail tucked tightly between his legs, his head lowered down and his ears pulled back. I stop beside him, carefully reaching for my sword, preparing for whatever we are about to face.

The trees on the side of the road were perfect cover for anything, with the high grass hugging tightly around their stumps. Rustling comes from the tall grass and I take a deep breath, focusing on where the rustling is coming from. My mind went straight to thinking it is one of the cougars with the long teeth, and this would be a fight for which I would need more than just my sword if I am going to survive it.

I put back my sword and draw the pistol Maggie gave me. My hand shakes slightly before I take another deep breath to calm myself enough to concentrate. As I am about to shoot in the direction the rustling was coming from, I see the long, large head of a giant 4-foot iron hide.

Iron hides, according to the homemade book Bex gave me, are what you could call a close cousin to the armadillo. Although they are probably just a genetically designed version of the armadillo, I hope there were still normal armadillos out there somewhere.

The iron hide slowly and casually walks across the street and shows little to no interest in us at all, its armor glimmering in the light. Unlike a regular armadillo's leathery armor, the iron hide has steel in its place to help protect it better than the leather would. People claim the iron hides are science experiments, which is why they have metal instead of leather. If that is true, which I do not doubt for a second, I feel sorry for them but, at the same time, I know with this alteration they are a lot better off.

There is a very short list of things that can kill it which makes it, in the long run, indestructible.

After the iron hide disappears on the other side of the road, Kota and I continue walking forward when we come across a two-headed deer with one of the largest sets of antlers I have ever seen intertwined between both of the heads. As we get closer it quickly runs off, more afraid of us then we are of it.

When we finally find a city, right away I wish we had not. All of the residents who had once lived here had been turned into disgusting zombie-like creatures the book labels freak-a-zoids. The creatures walk and sound like zombies, but they have a large skull and black, alien-looking eyes. Best description I can give is someone attached an alien head like the ones you see on those shows about area 51, on a decomposing corpse.

Once one spots me with its long, bug-like eyes, it slowly drags itself in my direction. Thinking quickly, I shoot it in the head with the gun that is still held tightly in my hand. I was grateful for how big of a target it offered , considering I had never shot a gun before. The only problem with using a gun though, it echoes through the ghost town and notifies the other freak-a-zoids of my presence there and sends them all in my direction.

The whole city wakes up, thanks to that one shot. Putting the gun away, I pull out the sword and begin to take the creatures out one at a time, leaving only their bodies in my wake as I begin to clear a path.

A yelp comes from behind me which draws my attention to a freak-a-zoid trying to attack Kota. I glare to the creature and quickly decapitate it with one swift swing of the blade.

"Stay close," I whisper to Kota before I kick one of them out of the way. We continue to walk carefully through the town while I act as though this attack has not phased me even a little bit.

The more south we walk, the more heat there is. We constantly stop to drink water. I know we are going to run out of water soon if we do not stop somewhere. A large billboard ahead of us proclaims that, in the distance, the Great Sand Dunes will be visible. I smile, relieved to be so close to somewhere that should have water available. I regret my decision in not getting some from the little town we had passed earlier.

Past the large sign, I can see endless sand with mountains far off in the distance mocking me and, before the sand, I can see a long river that separates me from the dunes. In the distance, deep between all of the dunes, there is a settlement with homes and what looks like a large statue, all made of the sand from the dunes and the water of the little river. Maggie did warn us of a group called the followers of the Glowing One. She also said they were out this way. If that group is them, surely they can't be as bad as she said they are, could they?

Building up a little courage, I begin to walk towards the dunes. Every fiber of my being tells me to walk in the opposite direction, but I had to ask them if they knew how much farther it would be to get to Genesis. At the river, I quickly fill my canteen, praying the water isn't contaminated, and put it in my backpack before crossing the river.

Iron Heart

The water feels refreshing, even though the sand makes the river bottom feel like you are walking in mud. If I stop moving it, will cling to my feet tightly, desperate to keep me locked in its grasp forever.

Once on the other side of the river, the small shacks made from the sand become clearer. A large fire resides in the middle of it near the statue that has been made to resemble one of the freak-a-zoids. Only for some reason this one is smeared by some sort of radioactive material, giving it a slight glow.

I make a mental note to avoid the statue, as to avoid any and all of the radioactive material coming from it.

The hair on the back of my neck stands on end as I turn to look behind me across the river. It feels like someone or something is watching me but, other than Kota, I am completely alone. Shrugging off that feeling, I make my way towards the small camp with the large glowing statue of a freak-a-zoid.

The closer we get to the camp, the more I notice this camp has a lot more people than I had originally anticipated. The people, all dressed in green robes, kneel around the statue. A single man standing in front of them speaks loudly with his arms raised above his head and, unlike the others, his robes are light green, and glows as though it has been drenched in the same glowing substance on the statue.

Maggie was not kidding about these people; they all seem like they have breathed in a little too much of the radioactive material surrounding them and, in turn, it has warped their sense of sanity.

"Welcome traveler," the man with the glowing robes speaks cheerfully, as he draws my attention away from my inner thoughts. "What brings you to our camp?"

"I am just passing through." I eye the strangers as they all turn their attention to me.

"No, there is more." He gasps as he moves through his kneeling followers. "You seek to find something. No! Someone." His followers gasp in awe of him and his infinite wisdom. When the reality of it is he is just a man who just so happened to guess something generic, and then point out the obvious. Like a fortune teller, only instead of wanting money, he sought power from these people crazy or stupid enough to believe him.

"My twin sister." I hesitate to give him too much information about myself but, if I want to find Alise, I know I have to play along with these people and their over eccentric imaginations.

"A twin! The prophecy, my brothers and sisters!" He raises his hands again like he had been doing when I entered the camp moments ago.

"Prophecy?" I question as I watch the follower's reactions. Something did not seem right, and something is telling me I should run before it is too late but, at the same time, another part of me wants to see this through and what they think they are about to accomplish.

"A twin will come to us, and sacrifice themselves to the Glowing Lord. If our Glowing Lord lets the twin live, we will help them fulfill their mission." As he speaks these words, the followers quickly gather around me taking my backpack and sword before holding me firmly in place.

I knew I should have listened to my gut. The realization sets in as I look over to Kota, who sits quietly behind the crowd, out of sight and out of mind for the followers. *They did not even see you, did they?* He stuck out his tongue and panted slightly as he watches. *You little ass.*

The followers of the Glowing One lead me to a wooden-fenced pen, while dramatic drums begin to play in the distance behind me. The whole village gathers to watch, circling the entire fence.

I scan the crowd. They all seem to be whispering about something while I am forced into the empty pen. The followers who brought me into it quickly leave and I realize I am in here with what looks like a box or possibly a cage covered up by some sort of fabric.

The drums stop abruptly as the leader of this cult makes his way to the front of the crowd and starts to speak once more. "Brothers and sisters! The time of the Glowing One is at hand. Our Lord was created by the Atom and came to us to lead us to glory!"

The followers begin to cheer as I stand in the pen quietly. Making a trip here had been a mistake and a waste of time apparently. I turn my attention to the crowd, and spot Kota sitting among them, unnoticed yet again, his tail wagging happily this time. I make a mental note to deal with him later.

"Now, the twin from the prophecy has come to us at last! Brothers! Bring our Glowing Lord forth so he may decide this woman's fate as the prophecy declares!" The leader in the glowing robes raises his hands as the drums begin to beat again, louder.

Soon chanting comes from the crowd, which to me sounds like a bunch of gibberish a baby could do better. I wanted to question them on how exactly this prophecy will work when they did not get a willing participant. I know I did not agree to become anything's or anyone's sacrifice.

The gate opens enough for one of the followers to run in and pick up the ropes attached to the fabric and, my guess, the cage. They hand them to one of the spectators on the other side of the cage before rushing out.

The spectator with the rope slides off the fabric and slowly opens the door with the second rope.

As the gate opens slowly it reveals one of the freak-a-zoids. It groans as it limps forward out of the darkness of the half-covered cage.

Once in the light, it becomes obvious some of this one's skin did in fact glow. Meaning it had come into contact with quite a bit of nuclear material, which covers all of its skin.

"My Lord! We offer this girl, this twin, to you as you foresaw long ago!"

I couldn't keep my mouth shut a moment longer, this game was getting ridiculous. I turn to the leader furious with his idiocy. "How on earth did he foresee this long ago? He's the freaking living dead? Key word: DEAD!"

Cheers came from the crowed as it fixes its buggy eyes on me, the drums beating again quicker this time. My heart races at the same beat as the drums.

Glowing drool drips down this creature's open mouth as it makes its way over to me.

Then, I do something not one of the followers of the Glowing One could see coming.

I shoot the "Glowing Lord" right in the middle of its large forehead.

Chapter 9

The shot echoes as smoke raises from the barrel of the gun and the Glowing Lord falls heavily to the ground. A glowing green liquid begins to ooze out from the bullet wound as a hush washes over the followers. The leader of the cult rushes through the crowd and into the pen.

He looks up at me, horror on his face, his voice quivers as he speaks. "You shot the Glowing Lord!"

"Did you honestly think I would have let that thing kill me? Not to mention, who sends a random stranger into an enclosed pen to be 'sacrificed' without checking them for other weapons besides a backpack and a sword?" I shake my head slightly as I nod my head to the gun. "Poor sacrifice tactics if you ask me."

"But you killed him," he stutters, the shock still visible in his vacant expression.

"Again, you really should have checked my person first before trying to sacrifice me to it. Unless you actually did intend for that freak-a-zoid to die." I realize quickly, perhaps I am being a little too harsh to these poor delusional people. I decide now may not be the best time to ask but, I clear my throat and change the subject. "So, I know this is a bad time but does this mean you guys will not be helping me find my sister?" I look at all the horror-struck faces in the crowd. And at Kota, who has been sitting there the whole time, wagging his tail as if to say, *I knew you'd be fine out there on your own.* I wait half a beat with no response and decide I have been given my answer. "All right, then. I think we are going to go. Uh, good luck with that." I casually point to the dead freak-a-zoid, and then to the leader who is clearly having a mental breakdown beside his fallen leader.

I walk to the gate and let myself out, past the shocked crowd, who move aside to let me through without taking their eyes off their leader and the dead freak-a-zoid. Kota catches up to me as I pick up my backpack and sword off the ground by the statue.

Thinking all is clear, I let out a sigh of relief before I begin to hear the cult leader speak loudly once more.

"Brothers and sisters!" he began loudly. "We cannot just sit by as the one who killed the Glowing Lord gets away! Who is with me?"

Cheers come from the followers behind me as the ground begins to shake with their running. I look behind me briefly to notice the whole village is a mob running quickly after me.

"Time to go." I look at Kota, who barks his response back to me. We both quickly run towards the creek where we had originally come from. I dive into the water and swim across to the other side, not even stepping into the mud once, should it halt the badly needed escape.

On the other side, I stand and watch the villagers come to a halt at the river. I had hoped they wouldn't come across, but it was difficult to tell for sure if they would or not.

We remain in a staring contest for a moment before they finally decide I am not worth their time. The followers turn around and walk slowly back up to their camp, grumbling a bit as they go.

I let out a deep sigh before shaking my head and turn, walking back to the road. I let out a soft whisper under my breath. "What a bunch of nut jobs." With no help from them, I decide I will just have to continue south and hope Genesis and Alise are in that direction.

~ ~ ~

For the first few miles, I constantly check over my shoulder, making sure the followers of the Glowing One did not have some hidden bridge they were going to use instead of crossing the river as I just did. Considering I had just killed their "savior," I couldn't risk them changing their minds and want revenge of some sort after all. In the end, revenge never came.

Ahead of us in the middle of some sand, I can see pre-war homes that look like they have not been touched at all from the bombs that had fallen all those years ago. The thought of possibly finding a decent non-effected place to sleep for the night gives me some form of hope and, if it isn't a good place to sleep, perhaps I could find something worth scavenging to sell to traders later. I have no form of money and I know at some point I will come across a place where I will need it. The real question, what do they use for currency now? Is it still pre-war money? Or have they changed it to something different that is easier or harder to find?

I come to a large fence where a sign is posted with large warning letters claiming, "DO NOT ENTER! Government testing site." Kota whimpers as I begin to dig my way under the fence.

I turn to look at him. "Don't be such a pup, it probably hasn't been used for testing in years." Kota continues to whimper more but reluctantly follows me under the fence. The farther we head in to this enclosed space, the more Kota starts to act unusual. I let out a slight sigh and turn to him. "Fine, you can wait for me by the fence. Once I finish exploring these houses, I will come back to you and we will just keep on walking." *So much for staying in one of these places for the night, I wonder what got into him.*

Without hesitation, Kota runs full speed back to the fence and dug himself out and under it before I can blink. He then turns and watches me as he sits down much more comfortably on the opposite side of the fence.

I roll my eyes at the dog before continuing to walk forward, even more determined to see what was hidden within this tiny town's walls. While walking, I hear a slight crunch from under my foot, but every time I look down there is nothing there at all; it blends into the ground so well, whatever it is. I lean down and run my fingers by where my foot made the crunching sound, which reveals a piece of what appears to be skin from a snake. I drop it instantly letting out a slight shiver. I hate snakes. Luckily though, this is only the skin of one.

Everything grows silent as I make my way across the shifting sands of the test site. My heart races as a sudden thunderous sound comes from below. The ground begins to shake as though an earthquake is taking place at this very second. I have no choice but to pause as I attempt to stand while the ground tries to sweep me off my feet. My heart is racing as the sand begins to move even more. Something is moving under it.

Thinking quickly, I turn and run back towards Kota, who is now on all fours again and barking at me furiously.

I try to run faster, but the sand keeps shifting and catching my legs as I move. I have to stop when the ground ahead of me explodes upwards to reveal a giant sand viper who has been waiting from under the sand for prey to enter its lair. Today, that meal just so happens to be me.

The snake coils up slightly, its large cat-like eyes stare in my direction. Its scales the same color as sand, which explains why its skin had been unnoticeable as I stepped on it. It raises itself up to be almost nine feet tall. I can only tell this because now that I know what I have been looking for, I can see some of its skin laying across two of the houses in that small town I had been so interested in seeing moments earlier.

It peers down at me, flicking its split tongue to locate me.

My breath is caught in my lungs as I look up at the snake and whisper to myself, "you have got to be kidding me." With an unsteady hand, I raise the gun to it and begin to shoot a few of the rounds. Unfortunately, all that did was piss it off. I kept shooting until I had emptied the whole clip into this snake.

It hisses as it reveals its two long fangs which, from where I stand, look almost as big as I am. It is getting ready to strike and I know there is nothing I can do to stop it. I pull out my sword slowly, I will not go down without a fight.

A loud noise comes from the north, revealing a military helicopter, which just so happens to have a machine gun mounted to it. As soon as it is in range, it begins to unload the machine gun bullets into the large sand viper and, unlike my pesky gun, is actually effective.

While the snake is distracted, I quickly make a run for it towards Kota and dive under the fence, back to the safe side once more. As I reach the other side of the fence, I turn to see the snake fall hard to the ground, its face directly in front of my own. I let out a gasp and brace myself as the ground shakes heavily from the impact of the snake. Once the shaking stops, I stand and slowly back away from the fence, my heart beating heavily as I stare at my reflection in its golden eyes.

I was so distracted after the snake attack, I did not notice the helicopter landing behind me. If Kota hadn't started to bark, I would have still been oblivious to their presence.

I begin whipping the sand off my leather pants as I turn and walk straight into James' chest. I jump back quickly and stare up at him. I feel slight panic as I try to contemplate a way to escape from him before he forces me to go back to Fort Exodus.

"We meet again," James looks down to me, his grin is that of amusement.

"I'm not going back with you to Fort Exodus," I warn as I look straight into his eyes, before turning to notice there are two guards and a pilot waiting by the helicopter.

"Yes, you will. I just saved your life from that giant sand viper." He places his hands in his pockets as he continues to smile victoriously.

"I had everything under control, long before you showed up with your goons," I protest as I nudge my head towards the helicopter.

"Not from where I was standing."

"Then move," I snarl and push past him. He quickly catches my wrist. I look at him furiously, my cheeks turning bright red as I look down at his hand tightly grasping my wrist.

"What exactly are you planning to accomplish out here, Jemma?" James' eyes focusing on my own.

I tug furiously as I try to free my captured wrist. I glare up at him. "Let go of me. I need to find Alise. I know about Genesis, and I know it is only a few miles south of here. I also know she is in there, I can feel it. I have to save her from them before it is too late. I also know right now, you are in my way. I don't care who you are or who you work for, I will hurt you if you do not get out of my way."

He slowly releases my wrist. "And what will you do if she doesn't want or need to be saved? What if she isn't this person you used to know anymore, Jemma? What then?"

"She is and will always be that person I know. She will come with me. I know she will." I begin to walk down the road, Kota skipping by my side.

"Jemma." The way he says my name echoes through my head, the way he speaks, it almost sounds like he is concerned about me. "It has been seven years since you last saw her. I don't think you fully understand things are not what you think they are. You only believe what they wanted you to believe." I wanted to ask questions, but that would keep me from getting away from him as quickly as possible. I was going to walk as quickly as I could with or without soldier boy's permission. He sighs softly, as I was making my way out of earshot. "But, if you are going to be this stubborn about all of this, I will take you there myself." James waves to the men by the helicopter and it takes off back to Fort Exodus. "Just promise me that, whatever you do, don't get your hopes up, Jemma. There are a lot of things you don't know, and finding Alise will force you to learn some facts about Lillian and Alise, as well as things about yourself you will not want to hear."

"Do you mean the cybernetic experiments Lillian was testing on us? Yeah, I already saw the lab, which is why I need to find Alise. To save her."

He lets out another loud sigh. He is fighting telling me everything but I knew he wouldn't. "It is more complex than just that, Jemma. I assure you."

"I don't know how anything could be worse than a monster who experiments on her own children." I slow my pace and look up at him. Anger fills my eyes.

"There are far worse things. You will see and I promise you, you will not like it. I just hope you do not regret this, attempting to save Alise, and finding out the truth."

The conversation ends and has left me with more questions than answers. What is James keeping from me? What does he know about my family that I do not? Could it really be so terrible I will regret my choice in finding them in the first place? I guess I will just have to wait and see for myself.

Chapter 10

James and I walk in silence. The whole way it felt like he only came along so I wouldn't get killed before he could return me to Fort Exodus. I hate this feeling like I am being babysat. I left the bunker and survived the freak-a-zoids in that one town, not to mention the followers of the Glowing One. All on my own. I know I can handle whatever was about to come next on my own too.

"We should stop here for a little bit." He breaks the silence as we enter a small town that appears to be abandoned.

I turn to him. "You can stay here if you want but I am not tired yet."

"Look, we still have quite a ways to go and I'm hungry, and I just so happen to know that if I am hungry, so are you. Have you not even noticed your dog has been whining for the past half an hour?" He raises his brow to me as he turns my attention down to Kota.

I sigh softly. I had not noticed Kota's whining. But now that it was brought up, I could hear my own stomach rumbling which causes Kota to tilt his head at me.

The town is eerie and quiet, like all the towns I have come across so far on this journey, but I know by now quiet is never a good sign.

Like clockwork, freak-a-zoids begin to limp out of their hiding places. James begins to shoot them until his gun jams. Rolling my eyes, I take out my own gun and pull the trigger. The gun clicks slightly. I forgot I used all of the ammo on that snake, until I aim it at one of them and all I hear is the gun click repeatedly.

As one of the freak-a-zoids limps closer, I whip the gun hard at its face. It falls over, slightly stunned, which gives me enough time to grab my sword and slice through its head with ease. More of these monsters limp their way over to me and, as I did the first, I slice my way through each of them as well. The final freak-a-zoid falls from my blade, making this small town quiet once more. I kick a few of the bodies out of the way, retrieve the gun I threw earlier and place it back into my backpack along with the sword.

James, clearly in shock, stares at me, jaw dropped and mouth wide open.

"What?" I blink curiously to him. "I was out of ammo." I step over one of the bodies and continue to walk through the town, Kota right behind me.

"How did…? When did…? Where did…?" James shudders as he takes three long strides and catches up to me.

"I can say the trainer in Fort Exodus was not completely useless. I always just pretended to be bad at all of it and not pay attention. I actually learned quite a lot from her. Don't tell her I said that." I can tell James has come to a complete stop but, to my surprise, he begins to laugh. I turn and raise a brow and see him doubled over with laughter.

"How you described your training and how you were only pretending that you were not listening reminds me of myself when I was a recruit in the army." He shakes his head, chuckling more.

"Like you?" How James and I could ever be alike is impossible to fathom. He is an army brat and so irritating.

"Yes, when your father was training me, I was every bit the brat you were. I constantly was getting in trouble and causing all kinds of mayhem for him. Now I never tried to blow up Fort Exodus, but I did other things."

"Lillian never spoke much about him or anything he did workwise." I frown as I turn away from James and continue to walk down the road until I spot a diner and walk inside.

"Well, she also never really knew that side of him either, not like I did. The way you and Bexie were, that was me. It would drive Aaron nuts. I recall on many occasions doing something spontaneous to drive him slightly crazy. Whether I snuck out or I put black paint on his binoculars and ended up with permanent glasses until he noticed it. I guess I never realized how hard I was on him in the beginning. In some ways I think Aaron got his revenge in his own way. It had never really hit me until I had spent so much time trying to keep track of you after bringing you to Fort Exodus." We walk over to a table where I pull out three cans of food and pour one can into Kota's dish before opening my own and eating the food slowly. "The day Aaron died, he asked me to look after you and Alise but, with him gone, it was hard to even go to the house he had built because every time I was there, I saw him."

"Why come for us then? What was the point if all that did was pain you in the memory of Aaron?"

"Because, at the time, I was following orders. Once you were in Fort Exodus and I saw the rebel in you, it irritated me to no end. It was then I realized how like me you truly are. It brought back all of the good times I once shared with him, when I was not much older than you were when I brought you to Fort Exodus. It was rough in the beginning for Aaron and me, because I was an army brat, but in the end it helped to shape our relationship. I saw Aaron as the father figure I never had as a child. He did not truly die though, because his personality somehow rubbed off on you and me and, for that, I am somewhat grateful." James eats his food quietly and I watch him.

I thought quietly about what he said about Aaron and him. I will never fully believe James and I would ever have anything in common, let alone being similar in ways when we were both younger. But even so, it almost felt nice to know a little bit about Aaron, even if it is only in James' memory, it is something I did not have. I barely remember him. Seeing this more sensitive side of James also gave me plenty to think about. It made me wonder what his childhood must have been like. If he saw Aaron as a father figure over his own family, perhaps he had more to him than what meets the eye.

~ ~ ~

Mesa Verde is known for its ancestral cliff dwellings as well as the archeological sites; the prime location for someone who is fascinated with history. With scientists constantly looking to explore such preserved locations, it is clearly the perfect spot to hide a giant science facility. Homes are carved into the mountain giving extra places to stay if they decided not to remain underground, but desert nights are worse than the days with the temperatures dropping to below zero.

"I don't see any guards." I scan the cliffs slowly with a pair of binoculars.

"There are none at the houses on the mountains. They will all be placed by the main entrance to Genesis. As well as in Genesis with the scientists."

"So, if the guards are guarding the main entrance, how are we going to get down there exactly?"

He points to a small spot across from us. "Do you see the circle in the middle of that group of houses? That is an emergency exit, which should lead us down to one of the labs. If we take that route, we should be able to avoid the guards all together, as well as the security cameras."

"Great, I always wanted to jump blindly into a hole which is full of scientists and their experiments." I sigh as I stare at the hole.

"Well, it could be a whole lot worse," James adds as he slowly stands, whipping the dirt off himself.

I shrug as we walk towards the cliff face, slowly ascending the stairs to where the homes are located. The circular spot we saw far away turns out to be an archeological dig location that had been put out of use years ago, and is the perfect size to be used as an emergency exit.

"Tell your dog to stay. We have no way to get it down the ladders without taking up more time that we don't have," James orders as he stands by one of the wooden ladders.

"Kota, stay here. Find somewhere safe to stay until we can return." Kota stares at us as we slowly go down the ladders. It is not until we were over half way down when he begins to whimper and cry loudly above us.

"Shut it up!" James whispers furiously as he looks up to me. "It will give away our position."

I sigh and climb back up after we reach the next level and look straight into Kota's eyes. He wags his tail happily. I gently pet his head then start back down once more when again, his whimpering starts. "You have got to be kidding me," I whisper furiously at Kota.

James, grumbling. Climbs up the ladder and picks up Kota so his paws were over James' shoulders, descending the stairs once more. "Your dog is something else, Jemma." He strains to speak as he climbs down the ladder.

I shake my head and chuckle slightly as James passes me. Kota sticks out his tongue and wags his tail, which hits James repeatedly in the face. Once at the bottom, James puts Kota down, his face flushed slightly. I lean against the ladder and smile at him.

"Don't you say a word." James shakes his finger at me me furiously.

I raise my hands innocently as I laugh out loud. I lean over and pet Kota behind the ears. "No one would believe me if I did."

Chapter 11

James is right. We enter a door to Genesis, into what appears to be a dark lab. Kota instantly starts to whimper and plops himself down on the outside of the door as if to say, *I will wait for you here.* With our inability to see, we feel around and I groan as I bump right into a large metal cage. It is not until James turns on the light that I find myself face to face with a cougar, its golden eyes fixed on me, its long fangs dripping with saliva. The drawings did not do this creature justice.

James comes over and taps my shoulder which causes me to jump. He nudges his head towards the door. Nodding, I follow him out of the room. I turn to look behind me at the cougar, who paces back and forth behind the bars of its cramped prison.

In the next room we see a spikupine, which is the five foot porcupine with the quills the size of swords. I was warned about this creature too. Lucky for us, it is behind a thick layer of Plexiglas.

The more animals we see, the more confused I become. I turn to James. "I thought all of the creatures out there were created thanks to the bombs. I am aware of the rumors, but they can't all be true. Can they?"

"That is what they want people to believe. Animal testing has been going on long before the bombs ever dropped. A missing animal here or there in the desert, no one ever questioned it. Then the bombs drop, and it gives the scientists the perfect opportunity to release their creations, testing them once more with the radioactivity the bombs had so willingly offered them. Releasing the creatures into the wild at the exact moment the bombs fell gave everyone the only reason people needed to believe these new creatures came from the bombs. When in reality, they had been around far longer than that, and no one is the wiser."

"How could they get away with this? Why do this and release these creatures?"

"The government agreed to turn a blind eye, if..."

"If they create super soldiers," I finish James' sentence for him, slowly forcing the words out.

"Yes." His voice is saddened by this truth.

We fall silent for a moment as we leave the animal testing labs and walk down a bright hallway, carefully keeping our eyes open for guards. A large fluorescent sign above me states there is a cybernetics lab though the double doors ahead of us.

"If Alise is anything like your mother, she will be in there," James speaks softly as I wait, staring at the double doors, fearing what I may find on the other side.

After a brief pause, we walk through the double doors where new signs points us to the cryo chambers on the left and a testing lab to the right. I turn left and walk towards the cryo chambers, stopping suddenly as surprise covers my face. I see rows upon rows of cryo chambers before me and most of them are occupied.

I walk over to one of the first ones and peer inside it. The girl in the chamber stares blankly ahead of her towards me. She has long blonde hair and soft porcelain white skin, and her eyes also have heterochromia, only hers are blue and hazel. Unnoticeable at a quick glance, but if you take the time to get a really good look at her, you can see it. She is clothed in black leather pants and a black shirt. I turn to look up at James who walked up behind me to look at this girl as well.

"Why is she in this chamber?"

"Remember how I said the government only agreed to the animal testing if they created super soldiers?"

"I remember, but how can she be one? She looks no different from you and me."

"She is more different than you think. They say even though these super soldiers can do everything a human can, there is one variable that is different. When exposed to emotion, most super soldiers have none or are very limited to it. They show what they have learned but nothing more. They are meant to follow orders, showing they can do so fifty percent better than a human most of the time. Which makes her that much more dangerous."

"How could she be more dangerous?" I look to this girl again who looks no older than I am.

"How can't she? Say someone wakes her up with the correct command. She could have the whole state of Colorado destroyed before you finish the order you give her and, what's worse, she would not even question you as to your motive. She would just do it. Where a human would genuinely question the motives to destroying a whole state."

The door behind us opens and I see in the reflection of the glass there is a young scientist walking in towards us. Her hair up in a bun on top of her head and a clipboard tightly grasped in her hands.

"You are not supposed to be in here," the young scientist proclaims with confusion to her voice. I slowly turn around and a gasp comes from her before I get a chance to get a good look at her. "Jemma?"

Blinking, I look at her for a moment. With confusion I question loudly, "Alise?"

"It is you. Look at you, you look so traveled." Alise looks so professional with her hair up and wearing the long white lab coat.

"Look at you, are you a scientist now?" A wave of relief fills me as I wrap my arms around her, but that immediately changes when she loosely hugs me back. Something is wrong. She faces straight ahead and quickly moves away from me when I release her, as if I am some stranger. Does she not even remember her own sister?

"Yes and no, I work on the digital networking of the soldiers." The way she is speaking makes it seem as though she is nervous about something. As if that is not the worst of it, she is avoiding making eye contact with me. Which was not normal at all for her.

"How is Lillian?" James breaks the sudden silence.

"She is good. She is the head scientist for the humanoid project after successfully creating the first one." Alise glances at me slightly before looking down again nervously.

"Really? That is very impressive, don't you agree, Jemma?"

I can feel him looking to me to say something, but I cannot help but stare at Alise. Something is off with her but I cannot place it. I can tell Alise is nervous about how I am staring, but I have to figure out what changed.

"Jemma?" James blinks as he shifts slightly behind me.

Then I notice something. "Are you wearing contacts, Alise?" I question, ignoring James for a moment.

"No?" She tilts her head slightly, her head still lowered.

"Yes, you are." I walk over to her and lift her head. "You have to be. You have heterochromia just like I do. Why would you put in contacts?"

Alise blinks anxiously as I stare at her eyes curiously. She opens her mouth to speak but the door opens once more, cutting her off. "Alise? Ah, there you are." Lillian enters the lab. Her hair also up in a bun. Her once dark auburn hair is now mixed with a little grey. "Who are you talking to?" She is smiling, but once she sees us her smile fades instantly. "James? Jemma?"

"Lillian." James speaks casually, his eyes remaining on Alise and myself.

"What is going on in here? Breaking and entering, James, which is low even for you. That is against protocol. What would Lieutenant Grey say to that?"

He turns his attention to Lillian and smirks slightly. "As if you are one to follow protocols. You don't follow them at all do you, Lillian? Also, Lieutenant Grey already knows I am here, and will do anything needed to complete this mission." James voice was bitter as he eyes her. "Also, I might add. I don't know what Aaron ever saw in such a cold, empty, corpse of a person."

Lillian's jaw drops and her face turns a bright red. She glares at him and prepares to start yelling at him for his harsh words. Only I speak first, furiously. "I deserve some answers!" As I yell, Alise jumps slightly back away from me. *Why are you so afraid of me?*

James and Lillian stop and look over to me, both noticing I am getting irritated with the nonsense.

"Yes, of course, what do you want to know?" Lillian softens her voice as she walks over to Alise and places a hand on her shoulder, while smiling at me.

"First, I know about the lab in the old house. I also know you were working on some sort of cybernetic experiment, as well as using your work on Alise and myself. What was Alise talking about when she said a successful humanoid? In the paper it spoke about you doing cybernetics, is that referring to humanoids? My final question for now, I know Alise had heterochromia just like me, so explain to me why all of a sudden she doesn't and claims she is not wearing contacts?"

Alise looks nervously at me before turning to Lillian, who gives a look of *I will handle this.*

Lillian takes a deep breath as she begins. "I supposed you would want to have this conversation at some point in your life. There is always research out there about how if one twin dies, the other will either get stronger, or it too will die. Alise had a true twin who passed away during birth. The loss of this twin made her weak, causing her to have to spend weeks on end in the hospital. I came up with an idea to help her. With plenty of research and training in cybernetics, I used some of the genetics from her to help keep Alise going while I worked day and night to create a humanoid to take the place of the twin she had lost. The first few attempts failed, so I had to keep tweaking the code and made it so this next one could grow, learn, and believe it was in fact a real human being. Even with all I did, there was one thing which kept this humanoid from being all it could be: a heart. I gave it an iron heart which made it stronger but it also made it cold but, as soon as it was placed with Alise, it had a bond with her instantly. It helped the creature put down its tough exterior and even made it long to forever protect Alise, no matter what. When first introducing Alise to it, I asked her to wear contacts so it would believe they were both in fact twins."

"That humanoid, is it...?" I start to say, slowly putting the puzzle pieces together in my mind.

"Yes, that humanoid is you. You both bonded so well, and Alise was getting better, healthy even. I was so grateful. If it was not for you, Alise would not be alive today. That has to mean something, doesn't it? I lost one baby. I couldn't lose Alise too."

I blink as I stand there in silence, taking in everything I have just been told. I now understood why I have always been the way I am, but knowing no one would have told me had we not come here is a bitter pill to swallow.

"Jemma?" Lillian breaks the silence, her voice soft and caring.

"Did you know this whole time?" I try to mask my anger as I turn my attention to Alise. "Was this all a game for you?"

"Jemma, she was sick. What else could we have done?" Lillian began to argue with me.

"Did you know this whole time?" I ask Alise again as I narrow my eyes on her.

She nods her head slowly, refusing to look me in my eyes. "Yes, I knew about it. But no, I did not think it was some game to play on you. I wanted to tell you."

"You were my sister. I thought we told each other everything. I guess I was wrong on both accounts, wasn't I?"

"Jemma, I tried to give you a normal life, didn't I? To me, you were always one of my little girls."

"That is bullshit!" I snarl as I stare at Lillian furiously. "My entire life is a lie. The only time someone didn't lie to me was when I was in Fort Exodus." I pause, recalling Bex and all of the other "children" in my training class. I turn to James. "Are they…?"

He nods his head slowly, confirming the answer I had already known. They were humanoids, just like me.

"You have to understand, we did all of this for you. We did not want to hurt you by telling you that you are different."

"The thing is, I don't understand any of this. Everything I have known all this time is a lie." I let out a slight laugh as I shake my head. "Doing all of this for me because you didn't want to hurt me? Please, you did all of this for your own selfish reasons. It had nothing to do with me. You kept this front on so I would be forced to save her. You didn't even give me an opportunity to make that decision on my own."

"James, talk some sense into her, please." She begs as she looks at James with saddened eyes.

"Honestly, I think she is dead on. Aaron never liked the idea of leaving Jemma in the dark about what she truly was but you didn't want to tell her. All because you were afraid this humanoid you spent years making would refuse to help when the time came to it. What's worse is you also got Alise wrapped up in this web of lies. That is pretty low if you ask me."

Lillian stands there, speechless, her jaw drops and she starts stammering. Alise stands beside her in tears, her sobs trying to force their way out of her mouth.

Chapter 12

"I think I have heard enough." I let out a soft sigh, quickly growing tired of the silence.

"What are you going to do?" Lillian questions as she wraps her arms around Alise.

I make my way past them and walk towards the door. "I am not sure, but I will figure that out eventually. What I can assure you of, however, is that it is no longer any of your concern."

As I walk towards the door, Alise grabs my hand, quickly causing me to turn to look into her bright blue eyes. "Please, don't go. You are still my sister, Jemma, whether you are human or not."

I stare deep into her eyes and whisper fiercely, "you have no right to ask that of me. I am nothing but a joke to you."

"That's not true." She begins to cry as I tug her hand off of mine and leave the lab, heading back to the exit we had come through. James slowly follows me out of the room, through the animal testing area and to the door that leads out.

Opening the door, I see Kota quietly waiting for us. I scratch his head before removing my backpack and head back into Genesis.

"Jemma, what are you doing?" James watches, slightly confused as I turn around and go back in.

"Just a little well deserved justice. If you don't want to be part of this, go out and join Kota, I am not leaving until I do this." I quickly open all of the doors which lead from the animal testing lab to the rest of Genesis. Once all of them are open, I walk to the cougar's cage. It paces back and forth, as if itching to be released from its prison at last.

With the butt of my gun, I break the lock then quickly get on top of the cage. James, noticing what is about to happen, closes the door to where Kota is and climbs onto the cage beside me.

Once James is beside me, I open the door. The cougar looks up at us, and its eyes glow as it growls slightly in our direction. It paces around the cage as it debates whether or not it is going to attack. We watch and wait as it slowly skulks out of the room and down the hall.

We listen silently. I did not want to get down too soon, should it come back in, deciding we are the better food source. Content we are safe, we climb down and enter the next room where we begin to let the rest of the animals loose, leaving the spikupine for last. I place a string on the doors of its cage and rush back to the door between us and our exit. Closing it quickly, before pulling on the string and letting this large and dangerous creature loose.

It makes its way to our door and stares at us for a moment, before turning and walking away in the same direction the cougar had gone moments before.

Screaming begins to come from deep in Genesis, one scream sounds like Alise. I look at James, deep down I know I should save her but at the same time, who would do this sort of thing to anyone else? The sirens in the compound begin to blare and James clears his throat and nods his head to the door.

"Let's go before the whole place goes on lockdown and we are stuck down here." He opens the door and I slowly step through it as I fight an inner battle on if I had in fact made the right choice.

We leave Genesis in silence. James picks up Kota and climbs back up the ladder as if carrying a heavy dog up a ladder was an everyday thing. I slowly follow. Shots begin to sound inside Genesis. Clearly some of the guards have finally gotten to the animals that have been released.

James and I stand at the top of the old archeological dig site, and I just look out at the area around us silently.

"What will you do now?" James looks at me as he breaks the silence.

"I don't know." I look into his eyes. "I suppose now that I know the truth, I should figure out who I am and what I have to do to rediscover myself."

"That sounds like a good plan, but realize you have already discovered new things about yourself in only a couple of days that you had not known before your journey."

I smile slightly. "That is true."

"If you still plan to continue to find yourself, I can join you if you want company."

My smile fades as I glare at him. "I don't need saving. Plus, won't your army buddies miss you or something if you are gone too long?"

"Oh, believe me. I know you don't need rescuing. They will be just fine without me. My orders are to protect you whether you need it or not. And from how I see it, I am doing exactly that. I will report in on my radio every now and then with updates and they will be content, no questions asked." He grins as he turns from me, placing his hands behind his back. "I do hope we run into another group of followers of the Glowing One though. I want front row seats for that experience." He turns grinning brightly at me.

I blink in shock as I see his smile. "You saw that?"

"I have never in my whole life seen such levelheadedness." He begins to laugh loudly as he shakes his head. "Their faces were an added bonus as well."

Grinning, I chuckle slightly shaking my head. I slowly begin to walk down the hill, James and Kota by my side. Whereever we will go next was unknown, but I was sure I would figure it out.

"So," James breaks the silence as we walk into the shadows of the mountain. "I did hear a rumor about a place somewhere up north that apparently is an untouched paradise. How do you feel about making a trip north?"

I ponder slightly at the thought before smiling. "Sure, why not." I slow down and turn to James, my face growing serious. "You mentioned you have a radio so that you can report in, correct?"

"To report in on, yes." James raised his brow slightly, curious as to what sort of insane thoughts were floating around in my head. "Why exactly is my radio all of a sudden something you, of all people, are concerned about?"

"Bex," I speak simply as I stare off ahead of us. "I would like to see her again, after everything that has happened." I gesture towards Genesis. "She is the closest thing to family I have. Is there anything you can do to make that possible without sending me back to Fort Exodus?"

James looks at me for a moment, before offering a kind smile. "I will see what I can do."

"Thank you." I offer a slight smile as we begin to make our way off of the mountain with all of the abandoned houses. Curious where we will find someone who may have some clue where this paradise might be located.

Chapter 13

In this world of devastation, it is said there is one spot that has been untouched by the bombs. Those who talk about it call it Eden, and it is our decision to go and investigate these rumors. To see if it is real or just some wild story they use to give false hope to the people who are left in this world.

Whether these stories are real or not, it is not going to be easy to find where this so-called Eden is located. Most say it is somewhere on the coast of Maine; that being said makes it the best lead we have. Maine will be our first place to look and, if it is not there, we will slowly search each and every state until we find it.

We begin our journey by walking back towards Denver, passing the towns and the sand dunes, only stopping momentarily to watch as a large herd of terrifying horses which are called Bonemares pass us.

These terrifying new versions of horses have their bones visible through their skin, blood is matted into their once soft manes, and eyes a milky white color. When they whinny, it sounds like a high-pitched scream, making them seem more like the pets of a Grim Reaper then wild animals. Even though these bonemares looked like something from nightmares, they are majestic and very peaceful creatures who don't seem to mind our presence.

James mentions bonemares are not a result of testing in Genesis, but an actual effect caused by the bombs. How they have survived with so little food is unknown to both of us, but they were here, and thriving and that matters more.

A bloodmare colt comes up to us curiously, sniffing us, as it is watched carefully by its mother. After investigating us it quickly runs off to rejoin the herd. Soon the whole herd is out of sight and we were able to continue on our journey back towards Denver.

We make our way to the Garden of the Gods again, hoping before we make this long journey to Maine that Maggie may have heard something about this mysterious Eden.

Maggie grins as she sees us entering the camp, she quickly walks over to us before we make a step into it.

"Welcome back!" With one arm she forces me into a hug that, no matter how hard I squirm, I can't seem to break free of. "We all heard about what happened at Genesis, those animals getting loose! I knew you'd make it out of there in one piece, not going to lie though you had me worried, you did." She turns her attention away from me and over to James. "And who is this warm ray of sunshine you brought with you, Jemma?"

James blinks slightly. He appears to have been caught off guard by the way Maggie was talking about him, and the look she is giving him causes his cheeks to redden slightly. He turns to me awkwardly, knowing I am enjoying seeing him squirm slightly by a swooning Maggie.

"Oh, don't you be shy now. My husband, rest his soul, looked just like you: handsome and muscular. I bet you know a thing or two about…" She winks at him as her eyes soak up his body. He awkwardly blushes, running a hand through his dark hair, while he gives one of his most dashing smiles and I can feel myself blush. There's just something about that smile.

"Maggie," I turn her attention as well as my own away from James for a moment. "You get a lot of travelers through here, right? Have you heard any talk about a place called Eden?"

"Pardon?" She slowly takes her eyes off James to look to me. "Eden? Was that the place that was supposedly untouched by the bombs? Many people have passed through here, you know. They said it is in Maine, but no one found it. Just stories I am afraid. Would be nice though if it had been true, don't you think?" She lets out a soft sigh as she shakes her head.

As I ponder her words, I don't trouble myself with who has or who has not tried to find it. What caught my interest is that she did not say it did not exist, but that no one has found it yet. That makes all the difference in the world. In the short time since I left Fort Exodus, I faced Lillian and Alise, as well as the freak-a-zoids, not to mention all of the other creatures in this new world. If I can do all of that, Eden does not seem impossible to find. It will be a long walk to Maine, but I believe that, if it exists, it will be worth it.

The night feels painfully long as I watch Maggie drink some "homemade" wine while she swoons more over James, who flirts back with her and even shares some of the bright red liquid. He often looks to me to make sure I had not left. Once he is satisfied I am still there, he turns his attention back to Maggie. I do not understand my own feelings, let alone if he actually has feelings for her or is just being nice. I feel a rage build up in me as I watch James. Why do I even care? James can have feelings for anyone. It should not bother me. Yet, for some reason, it does. I finally get up from the fire and mention that I am going to bed so that I will not be tired during our long journey the following morning. James agrees it is a good idea and that he, too, will retire for the evening.

James stays in a tent with one of Maggie's sons, while I stay once more with Maggie who is as talkative as ever, even though I have mentioned repeatedly that I need to sleep. I had not realized until I drifted off into a dream that I had finally fallen asleep in the middle of a conversation with her, Kota resting happily by my side. As I fall asleep I have dreams I am back in Genesis, but I am not me at all, I am Alise.

I could tell I was in Genesis because in the dream I was in the room with the cryo chambers. My heart was racing as I look around at all of the broken glass and the bodies of the humanoids that had been created here. The fluid from the chambers covers the floor. I feel my breathing pick up pace as the sound of screaming comes from deeper in Genesis. My whole body shakes as I look to my hands, covered in a large amount of blood. I don't feel injured, leading me to believe that this blood is not mine. It couldn't be. Panic sets in as I rub my hands on my pants, trying to get the blood off of them, but no matter how hard I try, it won't come off.

Why am I down here? What is going on? I clearly remember leaving Genesis earlier today, yet I came back. Why?

I leave the cryo chamber room and carefully walk down the hall. I pass mangled bodies every time I turn a corner; some have large sword like quills in them, and others look like they have been eaten alive. My heart pounds in my head as I keep moving forward through the hallway.

I come to a complete stop as my eyes meet that of a cougar's, its cold, gold eyes staring straight into mine and deep into my soul. I turn and run as fast as I can, but it is faster. I run into a room and slam a door between me and the cougar. It growls and claws at the door furiously.

When it finally stalks away, I let out a sigh of relief, but the relief does not last long as I hear something behind me. I slowly turn to see I am now face to face with the spikupine. I carefully reach behind me and slowly open the door.

It raises its sword quills. I scream at the top of my lungs as the quills shoot out towards me.

I jump straight up and run my hands along my body, checking for any injuries, but there are none. Kota lifts his head and looks at me, tilting it curiously before lowering it back down onto his paws. I slowly lay back down and attempt to sleep once more, while also trying to understand where these nightmares are suddenly coming from. James has warned me about dreams that might come from what happened today in Genesis, and not to worry too much about it. That is easy for him to say. He is not the one now facing these unwanted nightmares.

Chapter 14

For the rest of the night, I did not return to Genesis. It was more of a dreamless sleep that finally came over me, once I was able to fall back asleep. When the sun finally rose, I got up and joined everyone outside of the shelter as they moved about the small camp.

Kota ventures around the crowd of people as he begs for food, as if this is something normal and acceptable. Considering that was how he ended up joining me on my journey, I suppose it is normal and acceptable for him to do that now.

James was sitting at a table eating his oatmeal quietly while focusing intently on a torn map, one which was given to him by one of the traders here in the camp.

I walk over to where a large metal pot is full of oatmeal, and slop a few heaping scoops into a bowl before sitting across from James. As I sit, I notice he has not even touched his food. Knowing how he was back in Fort Exodus, he had clearly been up quite a few hours before I got up.

He looks up slightly at the movement, only to see it is me. "I have been looking this map over for the best route. I think the best way to go will be to move through Kansas and keep moving east until we reach New York. Then go north until we reach Maine." He moves his finger along the path he's mentioned. Kansas, Missouri, Illinois, Indiana, Ohio, Pennsylvania, New York, Vermont and New Hampshire, before tapping Maine once he reaches it. "What do you think? I also believe we should find a vehicle. It will be a lot faster if we can find one."

I stare down at the map, following the path we will take. "It looks like a good route. Where exactly do you plan on finding a vehicle to get us there? Not to mention, if we cannot find one, how long will it take us to get there?"

James eyes the map. "We can try vehicles abandoned on the road on our way through cities. Eventually we should be able to find something that works, until it runs out of gas then the search is on once again. As for how long it would take without a vehicle, it all depends on how many complications we face on the way. But, if I could guess, I would say it could take at least a month and a half, give or take a few."

"What sort of complications?" I question as I look up from the map into the face of an unusually shocked James.

"Really? You have been lucky all you have found thus far are freak-a-zoids and the followers of the Glowing One. There are groups of people out there who only want to kill, and it doesn't matter who you are. If you have something they want, whether it is land or just an item, they will kill you for it. Other groups will kill you just to kill you. Let us hope we don't run into either of them."

"We don't have enough ammo then, if those are some of the people we could potentially run into."

"You're right there, we will find some places on the way. The army has a bunch of abandoned bunkers that happen to be full of ammo, all across the country. The hard part is finding them." James rolls up the map and places it into his shirt pocket. "Good news for you though, I know where all of the good ones are." He winks slightly as he beams with pride which in my eyes seems a bit more like arrogance.

"Let's hope you are right. I would hate to run into a non-abandoned bunker, especially since you are supposed to take me back to Fort Exodus." He gives me a look of surprise. "Oh, please. I heard you radio them, explaining what you wanted to do. They told you to 'Stop following silly rumors and bring that girl back now.'" I smile slightly as I place my elbow on the table and lean into my hand, looking at him. My long hair cascades down in front of my left side slightly. "You don't follow orders very well, do you?"

"You are one to talk, Jemma." James retorts with a large grin spread across his face. He gets up from the table, takes his bowl of uneaten food and walks off.

I watch as he leaves, a slight smile of contentment on my face. Perhaps this soldier boy is not as bad as I had once thought. I gasp at the thought and quickly turn my attention to the oatmeal, as well as other thoughts of the journey ahead of us. I search for any sort of distraction to get my mind off what absurdity had just run through my mind. James is James, the jerk who practically kidnapped me when I was thirteen. The topic of traveling, as well as my thoughts about James, was beginning to make my stomach churn.

Kota, touching my arm slightly with his wet nose, catches me off guard for a moment. I turn my attention to him and he wags his tail happily. I place my bowl of food in front of him. I lost my appetite.

By noon, James and I are both packed and ready to start this journey to find Eden.

Maggie sees us off, waving as we go and reminds us what to look for and to come back soon. Considering word spread fast, there is no doubt Maggie will find out about us finding Eden long before we could come back to the Garden of the Gods and tell her.

Looking one more time at the camp, I turn my attention to Maggie who is holding some form of a cloth to her eyes as she cries slightly.

She waves once more to me, and I offer her a smile and wave back to her before I turn and begin to walk away.

As we move out of camp I hear her yell after us, "If you and Jemma don't ever decide to get together, I will be here waiting for you, handsome!"

James grins a sheepish grin as he turns to her. "I appreciate it, ma'am, but you are far too good for me." Maggie blushes and turns red before she giggles like a school girl and swoons some more over him. At first I am shocked by his comment but once we are out of earshot I begin to laugh loudly. I laugh so hard I have to force air into my lungs because I cannot seem to stop laughing.

We decide to walk to Kansas and begin our search for a vehicle there. At least then we will not have to head back into Colorado.

Chapter 15

We leave Colorado's landscapes, full of mountains, and enter Kansas; the land of nothing but flat lands, where you can see so far ahead of you, nothing will ever be able to sneak up on you.

James informed me that, before the war, all of the fields were farm lands with golden wheat as far as the eye could see. I stare out at the wastelands around us, wishing it could be fields full of golden wheat now but its long since died. Without landmarks or any form of anything around us, it feels like we are not moving at all. Even if we are in constant motion, there is no resolve and no proof we were making progress.

Dark black clouds begin to appear behind us, and threaten a thunderstorm sometime soon. We watch the quickly moving clouds as we continue to walk farther up the road.

In all of my years, I had never really seen many storms, at least not while I was out of the house. I stop and look up at the clouds as they begin to cloak the sky in darkness above our heads.

James follows my gaze as the wind begins to pick up and thunder rumbles overhead. "We need to find cover," he says, raising his voice over the quickened winds.

I turn and look at him, a grin on my face. "Are you afraid of getting a little wet from the rain? It won't cause you to melt you know."

"Considering the rain is now formed by radioactive water, yeah, I don't want to get wet. This rain is ten times worse than acid rain and I don't know about you, but I don't want to end up a radioactive freak."

Understanding the severity of the situation, we both begin to scan all around us for a place we can use as shelter. I have never been so grateful for all of the flatlands around me. "There," I call out as I point to a farm house sitting in the middle of an empty field surrounded by a small grove of dead trees.

James nods his head in agreeance there would be perfect.

A second clap of thunder rumbles overhead right before we begin to hear behind us the padding sound as the rain begins to hit the ground.

We run full speed for the small farm house, and barely make it onto the front porch before the storm is fully upon us. The rain hits the roof furiously while we stand on the porch and watch it fall around us. It quickly takes away all visibility, only allowing us to see the edge of the porch and no farther.

James, having seen enough, pulls his gun out and carefully opens the door to the house. The door creaks open, and he pauses as he listens for anything residing in this house. Hearing nothing, he opens the door more and searches the rest of the house.

I slowly follow after him. The house has two stories and, if you ignore the broken windows and the holes in the floor, it is still quite a nice little space to relax while we wait for the storm to pass. I look up at the ceiling and notice large holes revealing the room above. Above me a bed was sitting in the hole of the roof which gives me a sense of concern. All I can do is hope it will not fall on us during the night.

James returns to the living room carrying blankets he found on his adventures through the house. He see's slight concern on my face as I stare out the window. He places the blankets down on the damaged sofa. "We will be safe in here. The rain won't get through the roof, and if it does, the second floor will have to be ruined first."

I nod slowly, before making my way to the logs sitting by the fireplace and throw them in before lighting them with ease. The extra light the fire gives helps calm my nerves. If we run out of wood we will have to dismantle the dressers as well as the table and chairs.

Kota lays in front of the fire and slowly drifts off to sleep.

I almost fall asleep as well staring at the flames, until I hear James moving around as he starts placing something on the coffee table. "What are you doing?" I question as I turn my attention first to him then to the chess board and its pieces being placed in their spots.

"Want to play a round?" He nods his head to the chess board as he places the final piece.

"Sure, why not." I grab a chair from the kitchen and place it across from him, studying the pieces slightly.

"You first." He motions to the board.

I blink and slowly move one of the pieces before looking up at him. "Do you think Eden is real?"

He shrugs as he moves a piece slowly, not taking his eyes off the board. "Who knows? I want to believe there is somewhere out there not touched by this war. But at the same time, I am not getting my hopes up."

I move one of the pieces slowly. I hope this place is real for all of the people out there who have the same hope and believe that somewhere in this world of destruction, life from this Eden, could return this world to how it once had been. And, if humanity has learned from its mistakes, this will never happen again.

"Jemma?" James broke through the silence and drew my attention back to him and where we were. "Are you alright?"

"Pardon? Oh, I am fine. Why?"

"You spaced out there for a moment." He smiles slightly.

"I must be getting tired," I admit and stretch slightly while trying to focus on the blurry chess board.

"Get some rest, it is getting late. I will as well, there is no way anything will disturb us while that rain is coming down the way it is."

I nod my head, get up from the chair and pick up a blanket. Lying on the floor by Kota, I quickly drift off to sleep. As I do, my mind sends me back to Genesis once more.

My heart races and pounds as loud as drums. I look down at all of the blood covering my arms, hoping all of it is not mine. At the same time, I'm terrified it isn't. My body shakes heavily as I pull myself up off the ground, bracing myself on the wall. Limping, I make my way to the animal testing lab, knowing that was how I got into Genesis, it will also be my exit.

My hands seem weak as I fight to get a grip on the handle of the door. I leave a bloody hand print behind me as I push the door open.

I blink slightly as the fresh air hits my face. It's a welcoming embrace, only because the air in Genesis was beginning to smell stale with the quickly rotting bodies. I look to the ladder and slowly climb it until I reach the top.

Having completely exhausted myself, I sit and stare at the moon and the star-speckled sky. I am in awe of this moon tonight for some reason. It was like I had not seen the moon in years.

I begin to relax and get quite comfortable, happily enjoying the moon's rays. All is not calm though, as I hear the flapping of wings, a sound that should be all too familiar to me now.

I turn quickly and see the large bat hovering over my head. I let out a gasp before getting up as quickly as I can and limp my way into one of the abandoned stone houses. I limp to the far side of the house and curl up in the corner, staring at the door anxiously. A loud slam comes from the front door, which causes me to jump.

I jump up, disorientated, and look around the house frantically as I try to find the bat. I relax as I see James, already awake and making food for us from the rations Maggie had given us.

"Another nightmare?" he questions as he hands me a plate of food.

"Yeah, it felt so real." I let out a loud sigh as I take the plate from him.

"You had a big trauma; it is common to have that. I've known many soldiers who never could get over some of the things they saw when we were over in Europe."

"You wouldn't think I would have to deal with this, considering I am a humanoid after all." I put a spoon full of food into my mouth as I watch him make a plate for himself. Kota is already in the corner of the room slopping away at his food.

"When you were in Fort Exodus, do you remember all of those tests we did on you?" I gave him a glimpse as if to say I don't know. "Well, we were doing tests to learn more about you and what exactly Lillian had programmed in you. We wanted to understand and, from what we learned, you are just like a human. We learned you and all of the other humanoid children will grow up just like a human, you can feel just like a human and you can die just like everything and everyone else if you are not careful."

I blink as I look up at him and let out a slight sigh. "I wish I didn't get programmed with all of these hidden feelings, the world would be so much easier to manage without them. Especially since I don't understand half of them."

James lets out a slight laugh before eating some of his food. "Don't we all."

After we eat our dinner, I curl up on one side of the couch with the blanket tightly held to my face. Kota is resting by my feet and James stays in a chair by the fire and keeps it going. As I doze off, I catch a glimpse of him looking at me. In my dreary state I am not sure how I feel about him watching me. The annoying part isn't that he is watching me sleep like a creeper, it is the fact I feel safe with him watching over me.

~ ~ ~

The rain stopped half way through the night, leaving its own little path of destruction in its wake. A few of the trees surrounding the farm house had fallen over in the night, and looked like they had exploded upon contact with the ground.

I look out the window for a long time as I brush my hair thoroughly before putting it back up into a ponytail. I wonder how something as bad as a bomb could produce so many different dangers that are far worse than anything I could have ever imagined.

"How far are we planning to get today?" I question as I pack up my things before slipping my backpack onto my back.

"Well, if my calculations are correct, we should be able to make it to the world's largest ball of twine by noon. But that is if we don't have any issues as well as if we can keep up a good pace. Before we leave the farm, I want to check the barn and see if there is a working truck in there. If not, we will walk. It won't be a problem one way or the other."

"World's largest ball of twine?" I had stopped listening after I tried to figure out what this largest ball of twine could be.

James picks up his stuff and we walk out of the house around to the barn where there is a tractor, but it did not work. And he mentions that even if it did, it would be slower than if we walk.

We make our way down the road towards this ball of twine, whatever that is. As we walk, James takes it upon himself to give me a history lesson, considering I made the mistake to ask him what it was.

"Back in 1953, a farmer, like many in that time, saved bits of twine by rolling it into a ball in his barn. Instead of using it or getting rid of it, he just kept it and added on to it, piece by piece. By 1957, the twine stood at eight feet tall."

"Eight feet? That is ridiculous," I look from James to the town that is full of freak-a-zoids. "Why did they make it a tourist attraction?" I question as I cut down some of the monsters with my sword. Just another day in paradise.

"I am not sure. Just because they thought it was cool, I suppose." James shrugs as he shoots at the freak-a-zoids I missed.

It takes us a few more hours than we expected to get to Cawker City, the place where the twine is located. We had been on the search for a working vehicle which, to our surprise, was so far not at all working in our favor. All of them were either run down or out of gas, with no gas station in sight. James suggested if we find a gas station, we should just get some gas and take it with us. I told him it was up to him, although if we did find one, he was carrying the gas.

As we walk down the streets in Cawker City, the street is lined with shops. My attention is caught by a faded yellow line going down the road.

"What is that yellow line all about?" I question as we walk over to one of the faded lines on the cracked sidewalk.

"That's a twine strip. At one time, the stores all had paintings in them with the twine somewhere in them to somehow commemorate the it."

"That's a little over eccentric for a ball of twine, if you ask me." My eyes scan the yellow twine marks on the ground, noticing they all lead to the shops, just like James had said.

He gave a slight shrug. "To each their own, I suppose."

The ball of twine sits in a slightly collapsed gazebo that, at one time, had probably looked very nice. As for the ball of twine itself, it looked weathered and frayed, the bombs and weather had not been kind.

James stares at it in silence, mesmerized by this large ball.

I quickly lose interest and walk over to what appears to be a gift shop. I slowly move down the aisles and pick up the souvenirs to study them. Once content with the ones I select, I slip them into my backpack for safe keeping. They would not be missed anyways. Why not keep a souvenir that may mean something to me in the future when I look back on this voyage?

"We should keep going." I walk up behind James who still has not moved from where I had left him moments earlier.

He softly nods, as we turn our back to the ball of twine and Kota quickly follows after us I turn to James, a slight grin on my face. "Bet one of those cougars would have a field day with that ball of string." As I turn to look at the road ahead of us again, I can hear James slightly chuckle at my comment.

As we make our way to Kansas City, thoughts of a cougar playing with the ball of twine keeps us mildly entertained for a short time. Both of us wondering, if it would in fact be a little too big for even them to play with.

Chapter 16

Kansas City, a city that is torn in half by both the Kansas and Missouri state borders. A city once full of tall sky scrapers, museums, as well as beautiful monuments and parks.

The war had not been kind to Kansas City. Some of the sky scrapers look like they have large holes taken out of them. They are inhabited by different groups of people who, according to James, we did not want to meet if we value living, considering they did not like newcomers in their town let alone in their buildings.

The sky scrapers that have not been inhabited, lay in piles of rubble and are scattered across the streets of the city, making traveling more difficult. You have to constantly watch your footing so you don't trip.

The parks this city was once known for did not exist anymore, and all monuments that had not been completely turned to piles of rubble were either broken or damaged beyond recognition.

At night, the whole city glows orange and yellow from fires that still burn far below the city. It is likely caused by some form of a natural gas main and, after the bombs dropped, helped to release it causing a fire to constantly burn bright.

Kansas City is nicknamed the City of Fire and seeing it in person, its nickname has been well earned.

James, Kota and I make our way through Kansas City. The eerie silence makes me feel slightly uneasy. We cross over the collapsed rubble of what was once a sky scraper, and find ourselves in downtown Kansas City. A dark river flows between it and the only thing that will get us from this side of the rubble to the other side where there is more rubble, is a long, broken bridge.

We already thought it was strange the city is silent, but that does not scare me as much as a river that is as still as this one.

I study the bridge slightly for a moment, before I begin to make my way to the stone stairs that lead to the water. I figure I can fill our bottles to boil later on in the day, but as I am about to step down the first step, James places a hand out to block me from moving. I turn my attention to him, irritation and confusion fill my facial features. I did not understand why he was stopping me. We need water.

"Do not trust still water," James spoke in a raspy whisper. His eyes focused on the water as he tilts his head to Kota, who is growling softly with his hackles up and his tail between his legs. He knows something is out there.

After the encounter with the large sand viper, I learned the hard way that I should trust Kota's instincts. I nod slowly, back away from the steps and follow James and Kota as we walk to the bridge.

The bridge has large chunks missing from it, which makes it a lot more difficult to navigate over. But we are grateful we have not found a vehicle yet, abandoning it here would have been a large inconvenience.

Kota runs all the way across before we even stepped onto the foot of the bridge. His tail wags as if he is offering encouragement.

Halfway across the bridge, I trip on some piece of rubble which sends some rocks plummeting into the waters below.

A large splash comes from farther down the river, which stops James in his tracks. He looks around at the water and listens intently. He looks from one side to the other, raising his hand slowly towards water on one side of the bridge. The water has begun to ripple as if something large is swimming close to the surface. James turns his attention to me and says, loudly, "Run!"

"What's going on?" I question as we begin to race across the broken bridge dodging holes and rubble as we go.

"Run!" James repeats.

We leap over a gaping hole in the bridge, moments before a large, long snout slams hard into it, which causes the whole bridge to shake. I turn long enough to see that what is attacking us is a giant alligator as it sinks back into the water.

We run even faster as the alligator again slams itself into the bridge at another spot closer to us. We barely make it across before it rams into it again. This bridge was not standing well on its own before the attack and now it finally gives up its fight with gravity and collapses into the river below.

We stare at the water for a while, my heart pounding loudly in my head. The water moves around for a while as the alligator thrashes through it wildly but, after a few moments, the water grows still once more.

"I told you." James is leaning over as he takes in large gasps of air.

"What was that?" I question as I turn and begin to move away from where the bridge once was.

"The alligator?" James questions as he begins to follow me.

"Why did it attack us like that?" I look up at James who is looking down at me, slightly confused.

"There probably is not much food around here for it. I know if a meal presented itself to me, and I was somewhere where meals were far and few between, I would have probably done that, too." James shrugs slightly. "Let's get out of here. We have quite a ways to go before we can really get a chance to relax. But before we do that, we need to find a vehicle. It is far too long of a walk."

"Where are we heading next?"

"Chicago. I heard a while back there is a large settlement there in something that was once an old mall. Perhaps someone there will be able to answer our questions about Eden; if it exists or if they have heard about a place like that."

We did not stay in Kansas City for the night. James found a jeep that somehow not only had not been damaged, but also had gas. He gets behind the wheel, and Kota and I sit in the back seat. Considering I do not know how to drive, and it is night, it is a good opportunity to get a little rest.

As we leave Kansas City, I turn and look out the back windshield and stare at the glow of orange and yellow that comes from the City of Fire. With a smile, I turn around and slowly drift off to sleep.

Chapter 17

The drive from Kansas City to Chicago feels like it will never end. I am grateful to not have to walk but, at the same time, with the number of times we broke down or ran out of gas, walking would have been faster, not that I will ever tell James that.

I blink as I feel the vehicle go over something, which causes the vehicle to shake heavily. I groan loudly. "What was that?" I look out the back window to see a freak-a-zoid laying exactly where we had just been driving. I turn quickly to look at James, a large grin on my face. "Did you just?"

James looks at me in the rear view mirror, a large sly grin covers his face. His smile fades as he turns his attention back to the road and notices the streets are filled with more of them than I can count. He slows the jeep down as he searches for a place to pull over.

I look out the windows, fear covering my features as I calculate the amount of them versus how much ammunition we have. "How are we supposed to kill them all? We don't have enough ammo, even if we have expert aim, not to mention if I use my sword there are still too many of them."

James pulls the jeep into a gas station where we watch and wait for some of the monsters to limp past. "We don't have to fight them for long."

I turn from the window to him raising my brow. "I'm sorry. What? What do you mean by that?"

He points towards what looks like a toll booth. "If we make it to that toll booth, we will be in Chicago. There are guards in that settlement I told you about who will help us."

I raise my brow as I stare at the distance we have to go on foot. With a slight sigh, I pull on my backpack and remove my sword. "Alright, let's do this."

James nods his head and we exit the jeep, giving ourselves away almost instantly to the monsters closest to us. I question why all of these creatures are here, and he mentions they travel to big cities in search of food. Just like birds once did during the winter, they migrate as well. Only instead of south, they move to where the most people will be.

We run through the large groups of freak-a-zoids until we are rushing past one of the toll booths, which has a large wooden sign propped up against it. In white paint it reads "The Mart Settlement" as well as "Traders always welcome!" After the words, an arrow points to the exit ahead of us on the right.

We follow the sign and take the exit. it leads us into the slightly less freak-a-zoid filled streets. The large buildings of Chicago cast long shadows bringing a chill to the air, I am not sure how long it has been since the day I left Fort Exodus but the chill in the air makes it feel like it has to be early November at least.

James had mentioned the Mart Settlement is made out of an old mall. What he failed to tell me is this old mall is the size of two full city blocks. And by the looks of it, has to be at least 25 stories tall.

As we get closer, we notice the founders who created this settlement used random parts of other buildings to build a giant concrete wall and, at its entrance, a metal gate to give people only one way of entering.

The amount of freak-a-zoids also decreased. Our guess is they knew better then to try and come for this settlement. Based on the body count we saw on our way to the gate, some had to learn it the hard way.

"Who goes there?" A voice calls from above us on the concrete wall.

James and I search around slightly before looking up at a man adorned in random items they must use as armor. "We are seeking somewhere to stay the night. Our names are not of importance to you. We have been traveling for days and our supplies are running low."

Silence comes from the guard on the wall. I stand there wondering if James saying our names were not important could possibly cost us entering this settlement.

James let out a gentle sigh. "We have been traveling for quite a few months. Please, allow us to restock and we will be on our way."

The gate slowly opens and we see the guard standing there as he gestures for us to enter.

James nods his head and leads us through the gate and into the small space between the Mart and the gate. I blink as I look up at the building which, to my surprise, looks like it has not been damaged at all in comparison to the places around it.

"So, where are you folks from?" The guard lifts his helmet, revealing he is at least in his thirty's.

"Denver." I turn to Kota and scratch him behind the ears.

"Denver? Wow, what brings you this far north?" He looks between us.

"We are looking for a place." I look up from Kota as I hear James clear his throat, and notice quickly he is giving me a piercing look as if to say stop talking.

The guard raises his brow as he looks between us. Clearly not getting any other information from us, he leads us over to the Mart's main entrance into the building.

As we enter, the first thing we see is stalls full of different traders in every direction we turn.

A sign ahead of us is a small map of the whole building, thankfully with labels in white paint to help you navigate this enormous settlement.

I stare at the people moving around the place as though it is a small city in itself. I have always believed there had been people who survived the bombs, but never in my life had I imagined this many.

The guard startles me as he speaks once more. "The first two floors are the market place. If you are looking for anything specific, that is where I would suggest you look first. On either of those two floors." He points casually to the map in front of us. "The basement is where the traders keep their livestock or animals. There is also a few gardens down there as well, you don't need to be down there though. There is nothing down there for you. On the third floor we have a medical wing. If you are injured, that floor is your best bet to get fixed up real quick. All of our doctors came from all around the world just to work here with us. Some of them have stayed, and some have left, but they all have very good reputations either way. There are bars on floors five and nine, and restaurants on four and six. Finally, the hotel lobby is on floor twelve, all of the floors above that are the rooms." The guard leads us to the stairwell and opens the door for us.

I stand there for a moment calculating before I turn to the guard. "What about floor seven and eight?"

"Storage," the guard speaks quickly before closing the door on us and walking away back to his post.

"That was strange," I mention as we begin to climb the stairs towards the upper floors.

"Don't get any bright ideas, Jemma." James turns to me, his face serious. "Your curiosity is going to get you into serious trouble one of these days."

I let out a deep sigh as we continue up the stairs. I slow my pace as we walk past floors seven and eight. I manage to take notice that both floors are guarded by two men who watch me closely as we move past. They appear to be in what looked like army-like outfits, but they were not army. How curious, I ponder as we move past the second set of guards.

On the next floor, I stop James and point down a floor. "Don't tell me that you are not curious! What sort of "supplies" need that many guards. Not to mention, in the middle floors of the whole building!? It makes no sense."

James sighs as he looks deep into my eyes. "Jemma, so help me if you even think of going in there, I swear I will tie you to a chair until we leave this place."

I crinkle my nose at the thought. Ew.

At the front desk of the hotel, James rents us a room with two beds so that he can keep an eye on me, hoping to prevent me from wondering off to the seventh and eighth floors. The woman at the front desk smiles as she twirls her hair while speaking with him, as well as laughs at all of his terrible jokes. I cannot help but feel my jaw drop at the two flirting. Kota huffs by my side and I let out a slight sigh myself before walking over to a chair by a fireplace.

James, grinning from ear to ear comes over to Kota and myself, a key in his hand and leads us to yet another set of stairs, which lead to our room. As we climb the stairs, he turns to me, still grinning brightly.

"Amy mentioned that if Kota needs to use the restroom, there is a 'garden' of sorts out the roof exit."

Amy? I raise a brow at James. What is this feeling I am experiencing? I have never come across it before, and especially not involving James. What the hell is wrong with me?

We put out backpacks in the room and leave Kota alone, which seems like no issue for him as he quickly pounces onto one of the beds and curls up happily.

We make our way to the bar on floor nine. James informs me that bars are one of the best places to find out all kinds of information, especially since bartenders often hear all sorts of gossip. Meaning they probably also heard about places most wouldn't know about.

The bar is dark and appears to be not too crowded. We quickly find ourselves a place to sit at the bar. We order food and something to drink while we wait for the few people who are at the bar to stagger out.

The bartender smiles as he wonders over to us and refills our glasses. "Haven't seen you two here before and I would know, I am really good with faces. Where you from?" His eyes are on me as he offers a broad grin while cleaning a glass with what looks like a dirty rag.

I push back my repulsion at the thought I have just been drinking out of a dirty glass. "Denver." I offer a soft smile as I raise my glass to my lips before recalling I do not want to drink my flat pop.

"Denver, huh? Were you close to that underground science lab that got attacked? Genesis, is what it was called. People are saying the experiments in there did not get out on their own. They also are claiming a person singlehandedly went in there and completely shut the whole place down. I heard there were no survivors. What a crazy world, huh?"

I blink as I feel a pang of guilt at the thought of no survivors. "Yeah, crazy." I turn my attention to James for a brief second before turning back to the bartender. "Did anyone ever say what happened to the person who did that? Not to mention what this person might look like?" I have to press and find out how much he actually knew. If they knew I was the reason Genesis is shut down, I doubted I would still be welcome here.

"No one knows who did it. Someone said it was the leader of the followers of the Glowing One, others say it is some new threat. Either way, no answer is ever the same. As for what happened to them, someone said they were killed by one of the experiments in Genesis."

I slowly nod my head. He knows nothing which is exactly what I want. The gossip has not been completely wrong, but part of me wonders how he would feel if he knew he is standing across from the person all those rumors are about.

"So, what brings you to Chicago?" He changes subjects as he scans the bar, making sure none of the customers need anything.

"Actually," James leans in slightly. "I was wondering if you could possibly answer a question of mine now." He offers a smile to the bartender.

"Of course, what is your question?" He looks between us curiously.

"Have you ever heard about a place in Maine called Eden?" James scans around us to ensure there are no prying ears.

The bartender curiously looks around then leans in closer to us. "A few people have gone to Maine searching for this Eden place but, as far as I know, none of them have found it. I hear talk that deep underground is where Eden is hiding, untouched by man. A true paradise."

"How far underground?" I look to the bartender.

"No clue. All I know is that Eden is marked by a lighthouse, but everyone who is anyone knows that there are at least 65 lighthouses in Maine alone." He shakes his head as he laughs slightly, before walking away to help a new person at the bar.

Content with the few answers we received, we make our way back to our room. I quickly hand over my leftovers to Kota while James takes out his map and sits down at the table. He is mumbling loudly as I sit down on a surprisingly well looked after couch, Kota quickly joins me after he finishes off my food.

"With 65 lighthouses, it could take quite a few days to figure out which one has the tunnel to Eden." James lets out a frustrated sigh.

"Then we will just have to go from one to the next until we find it. That's all." I run my fingers through Kota's fur, using this to help relax me.

From how I see it, there really is no way to know for sure how hard this task will be until we get there. We just need to remain positive and hope it won't be as difficult as we keep thinking it will be.

Chapter 18

James is up early the following morning and quickly leaves the room as he receives a call on his radio. He often does this when he receives calls from the army, it doesn't bother me though. So long as they are not making him take me back to Fort Exodus, I didn't care what the call is about.

He returns to our room a few hours later and lets out a slight sigh. "Looks like we are stuck here."

Raising a brow I sit up and look to him. "What do you mean we are stuck here?"

Turns out Maine is being hit by a hurricane, which meant it is far too dangerous for us to head any farther east until it passes. James spends more time on his radio and off doing his own thing that I have no choice but to keep myself occupied. To keep both Kota and myself from being bored, we explore some of the few thousand shops The Mart settlement has to offer. I trade some of my items I collected on my way here, for a new coat.

I have heard Chicago was labeled the windy city long before the bombs fell and, knowing it is fall, I want something to help keep me warm when I take Kota outside for his bathroom break, as well as giving me an opportunity to scavenge the area for more items to sell. If there is anything left.

After a while though, the shops become dull. They always have the same thing, they did not leave very often to get new items stocked, so it is like looking at the same thing over and over again. James is still off doing who knows what, and I never saw him come back to the room even once. Odds are he will return to it while I am out adventuring in The Mart, but still it feels strange not seeing him after all of this time when he wouldn't leave my side.

I decide one day to just stay in the room with Kota and look over the map James has, often wondering how much farther we will have to go. Concern fills me if the hurricane does not let up soon, we are not going to make it to Maine before winter kicks in.

I jump up quickly, which causes Kota to jump up too. We walk down the stairs and towards the entrance of The Mart. I smile as I spot the door, Kota quickly trots beside me, his tail wagging furiously. He knows we are about to go for a nice walk around Chicago.

"Hold it right there, miss." The guard we met a few days ago steps in between the door and us.

"Is there a problem?" I look between the guard and the door. Did James tell them to keep me in The Mart? If he did, I will find him and kick his ass.

"I can't let you out there." The guard's face is serious as he firmly looks to me.

"Why not? He has to go to the bathroom." I point to Kota, who whimpers slightly as he wags his tail.

"He will just have to use the garden out on the roof."

"Why can't we just go out here? I have no clue if he will be able to hold it with how many flights of stairs there are between here and the roof." I feel the irritation flow through my veins. "Speaking of stairs, how hard is it to have an elevator? Seriously."

"Elevators will take a lot of power from the generators, meaning, if we have them working then we will not be able to power the rest of The Mart. You cannot leave The Mart because we have been dealing with a torrential downpour which flooded the river and has covered the ground with at least one to two feet of water. The Mart is under lockdown; no one in or out." The guard lets out a sigh, making me wonder if he too was not thrilled about being stuck inside all of the time.

"How is it different if we go out onto the roof then if there is that much water?"

"There is a glass barrier around the garden to keep the rain out."

"How do you water your plants, then?" I rub my temples slightly. "Never mind. I don't really want to know. Let's go, Kota." We make our way back over to the stairwell.

An agonizing 25 flights of stairs later, we finally reach the garden, which is enclosed with glass just like the guard had said. The plants that were in this area had died some time ago, probably from their lack of being watered. I imagined it had once been beautiful up here, back when everything was still alive. Kota, not caring what this place looks like runs around the small garden space. I did not blame him; I knew exactly how he felt, having been left inside this huge building for who knows how many days now.

I make my way over to a bench and sit down on it, looking up at the glass roof, I watch as rain drizzles onto it. I can feel myself relax as the rain hits the roof. It sooths me and I feel myself drift off to sleep, my mind sending me back to Colorado.

The air is hot and I lift my hand to shade my eyes from the sun. Suddenly, a thunderous sound comes and the ground begins to shake. I turn and see the herd of bonemares running quickly towards me. I freeze, standing as still as I can while I watch them move quickly past me.

After they passed, I follow them until I reach the sand dunes where I run into the followers of the Glowing One, who seemed distracted since the last time I had seen them.

"Please help me." The words caught in my throat as I feel the words burn.

The leader begins to proclaim loudly about a prophecy, only this time it is about a girl coming to them for help, which they would only do if she sacrificed herself to their lord. Yet another Glowing One who they somehow found. Instead of taking them up on their "offer," I quickly run away. As I hit the water of the river between the followers of the Glowing One and the road, I jolt up. Returning to reality and Chicago.

The rain seems to have slowed down slightly, and Kota is now sitting beside me, confused as to why I have been sleeping when I could be adventuring the amazing things this garden has.

~ ~ ~

It turns out we have been here a total of four days, and it is not until the fourth day the rain finally lets up. Which means the water is slowly begin to go down, which also means we only have a few more days before we will be able to continue on our way once more.

Knowing we are still stuck here for a few more days, I decide to spend most of my time with Kota in the garden on the roof, only returning indoors for food and to sleep.

After not seeing James for a total of five days, he finds me on the roof one day, a serious look on his face. "Before we leave, I have hired a trainer to help get you in a bit of practice. So you do not get rusty, considering we have been safe and sound in The Mart all of this time."

I look up to him, a sweet smile on my face. "Trainer? For what exactly? I can still fight better than you do."

"You will get some weapons training, and a bit more hand-to-hand, as well as combat training. All of the reserves I had planned to get ammo from are apparently empty. We will have to be prepared."

I let out a slight sigh as we walk back to our room to get my sword and to put Kota in there while I am gone. "So that is where you have been?" As I reach for my sword, James places his hand on mine. Which sends a prickly feeling up my arm. I quickly pull my hand away from him.

"Hand-to-hand, not sword-to-hand."

I turn to him, a serious look on my face. "If this trainer hits me in the face with a ball of any kind, I will end you." I pull my long brown hair up into a ponytail as we walk out of the room.

"I highly doubt that." James shrugs as he smiles slightly.

I cannot help but roll my eyes. He is right, I wouldn't hurt him. By far he has been the most helpful person since I started this journey. I am not going to lie though, I hate that he is right. Probably as much as he hates all the times I am right.

The area where the trainer is located is on the tenth floor. James speaks highly of him, someone he clearly looks up to. So, I figure I will go easy on the trainer, considering they are James's friend.

I have a feeling this will be a dull session since I will be going easy on the trainer, but I suppose I will find out the truth soon enough.

Chapter 19

The training room is a wide open space with practice dummies, mats, and even large amounts of exercise equipment, which are located by the climbing walls in the middle of the room.

"Welcome, welcome." The instructor smiles brightly as he greets us. I blink in surprise as I notice quickly he is tall, very tall. He towers over both of us, which makes him at least six feet tall and, to add to that, he has more muscles than an iron hide has iron plates.

"Mark! This is Jemma, the one I was telling you about." James grins as we walk over. The way James spoke to Mark makes it seem like they are long lost friends.

"Jemma! Nice to finally meet you! James has told me so much about you." Mark sounds overly cheerful, which brings back my memories of Maggie with her overly cheerful personality.

"I doubt that." I scan the room, noticing there is no one else in the room except us.

"HA! Quick witted, this one, I like it. Very feisty." Mark grins widely.

"You have no idea." James smirks.

I roll my eyes slightly, already over the thought of training. "Can we get this over with so we can go?"

"Jemma!" James barks as he glares at me.

I raise a brow. "What?" I feel frustrated as I turn my anger on him, my hand balled into a fist.

"It is fine, James. Okay, Jemma, lets head over to the mats. We will practice hand-to-hand combat now. We can always save the talking until we are done." Mark grins as we walk over to the mats.

As expected, the lesson is nothing I have not already learned on my own. But to keep James off my back, I did what I was taught. It is too easy for me, and I quickly lost interest after getting the moves figured out.

James watches, seeing the boredom on my face, he calls Mark over to him and they whisper for a moment. Mark nods and leaves. "Let's go." James lets out a gentle sigh as he turns and walks to the door.

I raise my brow and run to catch up to him. "Really? That was it?" Something seems off. Is that really it? Some trainer he is. A child could have taught me those moves. I could not help but feel I have somehow upset James though. Did he know I was going easy on Mark?

"Yep, let's go." He continues walking without another look at me.

He is mad, I can tell. I let out a sigh and slowly follow, feeling defeated. The hair on the back of my neck raises as someone comes up behind me and places a sword to my throat.

"Where do you think you are going?" A voice comes from behind me. I feel my body tense up and my heart race quickly.

James turns to tell me something but the surprise on his face causes him to halt his words.

I slowly move my hands up to the blade of the sword, both sides sharp, I could feel it as I wrap my hands around it. The next few seconds, I move so quickly my assailant and James don't see my next moves coming until it is too late. I force the blade away from me, which cuts into the palm of my hands slightly but I manage to push it far enough away, allowing me to crouch down. As my assailant struggles to grab me, I take their arm and, using my bodyweight, I send them soaring across the two-block span of the room, and straight into a wall. I only meant to toss them on the ground. I did not realized I was that strong. I stare ahead of me at the wall where my assailant is slightly embedded into it. Behind me, James curses loudly. I turn to him, slightly confused as to why he is upset. I am the one who was attacked.

"What was that?!" James furiously points to the crack on the wall away from us.

"I was under attack!" I counter as I too point to the crack on the wall away from us.

"That was Mark! Jemma!" James has lost all composure and is yelling loudly at me.

"How was I supposed to know that!? I had my back turned to him!"

James wanted to yell more I could tell but instead he lets out a sigh. "Go to floor three and get one of the medics for him."

I want to keep yelling at him. How could he be so angry at me for accidently throwing Mark into a wall when it is his fault I had to do that in the first place? I have never been so humiliated in my life. Don't come up behind someone if you don't want hurt. I take a deep breath and walk down the stairs to floor three, still feeling heated because James yelled at me. I return with two medics who brought a gurney with them. Their faces turn from concern to shock as they see Mark lying flat against the wall, quickly they run over to him to help peel him off it.

"Sorry about that, Mark." James speaks to his friend softly as I reach them.

"It is all good, James. Definitely a feisty one, huh?" Mark grins as he tries to laugh, but begins to cough slightly.

"Yeah." James sighs softly.

"If I don't see you before you go, good luck finding Eden." Mark grins up to him. "And, good luck with her, too; you will need it." He attempts to laugh but starts coughing again.

"I am sorry about that. I didn't mean to." I look at the gurney he is on and feel a pang of guilt.

"Hey, it is my fault. Don't let this get to you. You are far more powerful than anyone will know what to do with." He let out a slight chuckle. "If James knows anything, he will know not to mess with you."

"That would probably be a good idea."

James clears his throat and gives a disappointed look in my direction.

"Sorry," I lower my head slightly.

Mark laughs loudly as he is carried down to the hospital wing. As he leaves, he yells back to us. "Take care of him for me, fireball."

We watch and wait a moment before James sends me up to our room, saying he will meet me there. I don't say a word, quietly walking to our room where Kota is waiting for me. He wags his tail happily as he sees me, I offer him a slight smile and slowly sit on my bed. It is not until this very moment that I notice that my hands are bleeding a lot more than I thought they could. Even so, my hands do not hurt, should I not be in more pain?

James enters our room, I slowly turn and look up at him. He looks like he is about to say something but instead, he goes over to my backpack and pulls out some bandages, as well as the disinfectant I had taken from the store months ago. He pulls a chair up to sit across from me and grabs a cloth. Without a word he carefully takes my hands in his. It almost feels like he cares, not that I fully believe that after getting yelled at a few minutes earlier.

I watch as he uses the fabric to slowly wipe off the dried blood from the palms of my hands. He watches my emotionless facial expression as he pours some of the disinfectant on them. I know I should be feeling something but I don't. The most I feel is sorry for what I did to Mark. I look up to James. "I didn't mean to hurt him." I turn my eyes back down to my hands as I watch him slowly wrap up my hands in the bandages.

"I know, it is not just your fault. It is mine as well. If I had not told Mark to try something like that on you, this would have never happened in the first place. For that, I am sorry I forced you into having to defend yourself."

I nod my head slightly, James finishes bandaging me up and gets up to clean and pack our stuff.

He turns to me, a grin on his face. "I did hear him bragging he had taken on five men and it was the sixth guy who finally got him. But, if he looks bad, you should see that sixth guy."

I let out a loud laugh at the thought of this wild story Mark has made to try and save face here.

Chapter 20

We leave early in the morning before even the guards are fully coherent. The events which took place the day before had not taken more than a few hours to spread. Soon the whole place buzzed about what happened to Mark. Mark's story about six guys attacking him quickly increased until there had been over fifty, and it was the sixty-first guy who finally did him in.

As we exit The Mart, we notice the weather is overcast and threatening more rain. The threat remains as we make our way out of Chicago and into Indiana.

James brought food that did not involve heating, that way we can keep walking and will not have to stop as often. It is almost like he wants to get this last stretch of the journey over with.

After three days of walking, we finally reach Ohio's border where a sign reads, "Welcome to Ohio! So much to discover!"

I eye the sign curiously. "I wonder what that means." I speak mostly to myself since I have no idea if James is talking to me or not.

"I guess we will find out." James grins at his joke.

I turn to him and smile. "Clever."

We walk straight until we reach Lake Erie, which we follow until we reach Cleveland. As we enter the large city, we can see all the worn down sky scrapers. I stop momentarily and admire one in particular; a half demoed building, in piles around it are large piles of metal and dirt. The pieces of the building that have not been demolished yet have some form of fabric draped over some of its roof, torn and waving in the wind.

The more I look, the more I feel like this is a crane cemetery, a little under a dozen cranes sit rusting from lack of care. One still has its operator, the skeleton's mouth wide open while its hand still grasps one of the levers that operate it.

Once content I have seen enough, we continue forward until we reach an odd looking building that has a gate wrapped around the entrances, but you can see through the gate at the broken orange bleachers.

"What was that place used for?" I inquire as I look closer at what looks like a field.

"Looks like some sort of sports field." James' tone is dry as he nods his head to one of the freak-a-zoids wondering in front of the gate wearing full football gear.

"What? Not a sports fan?" I curiously tilt my head as I look from the creature to James.

"I find the idea of recreational sport abhorrent. Not to mention, I would hate to run into a fan now in this world. They were bad before, I would hate to see them now."

I nod slightly in understanding which ends the conversation about sports. We quietly make our way past the football field, keeping the freak-a-zoids from realizing we are here in the first place.

We reach the outskirts of Cleveland and are forced to find a place to hide from the rain once again. We end up finding a strip of shops and bars that, at one time, tourists used to gather almost all year round.

While we wait out the rain, James looks at his map again at one of the tables in the abandoned bar. I look over his shoulder at the map. I find it hard to believe how far we have traveled to get to where we are now. Over half way across the entire United States, no wonder we are exhausted.

"It looks like if we keep following Lake Erie, we can slip through a small part of Pennsylvania and straight into New York," James points it out on the map as he explains.

"That seems like an easy enough route." I feel a pang of anxiety as I look at how close we are getting to Maine. What if, after all of this, Eden is not there at all? What if this trip was for nothing? What if, after all of this is over, James takes me back, or leaves me to face this world alone? I shudder at the final thought. How, after all this time, have I become so attached to such a… I can't even think of a word for him.

After all of this, I hope we did not come all of this way for nothing. Even feeling this way, we have to keep going; we have come too far to turn around now. I cannot go back. There is nothing left for me in Colorado.

Early in the morning with the rain stopped, we continue walking. No vehicles here seem to be working correctly according to James, and it will only slow us down if we keep searching.

"We will need to be careful once we reach New York," James adds as we make our way down the road out of Ohio.

"Why is that?" I look over to him curiously.

"We can expect a lot more freak-a-zoids there, more than anywhere else we have been so far."

"I am a little surprised we have not run into more recently. Especially since we just walked through Cleveland without seeing more than a handful."

"Oh, we will. Don't you worry about that."

"I am not worried, they should be, though." I grin at James triumphantly.

"That is the spirit." James grins.

Kota quickly runs behind us bringing all jokes aside as he barks loudly at us.

James pulls out his gun as I take out my sword, moments before we see a large horde of freak-a-zoids stagger their way towards us.

Chapter 21

New York, population of 8 million plus. Well there once was anyways, now, about 95% of them are freak-a-zoids.

We did not make it very far into New York before these monsters began to quickly climb, crawl and walk out of every building, destroyed or not, on either side of us. I look at James, concern covers both of our features. What were we supposed to do? If we begin to shoot, it will bring even more of them out but, if we run, we might live to fight another day. Although if we do that, we will still have to face them one way or another. There was no other way through New York.

James quickly decides to start shooting at them. We will fight our way through them.

I pull out my sword and quickly go to work on the group of freak-a-zoids ahead of me. Slicing through them quickly with little effort. Body after body falls. I slice through the last one and turn to look at James, both of us breathing heavily. I don't know how many I actually killed but it had to have been at least 100 if not more. Thankfully, they're not strong enough to fight against my sword and there's not much anything can be done against a gun.

"That was not so bad." I grin, quite proud of myself.

James points his gun behind me. "Don't get too comfortable just yet."

I quickly turn to see another group of freak-a-zoids flocking to the street. They had been drawn in by the noise we made. I rush the new group that have just arrived, and just when we thought we were getting ahead of it all, they begin to swarm.
I lift my sword to attack, but as I'm about to swing, out of nowhere, a loud explosion comes from right in front of me, which causes both James and me to stop. My ears ring loudly as I begin to feel dizzy.

Another explosion comes, and I find myself covering my ears as they ring even louder. James runs quickly over and is yelling something, but I can't hear anything he is saying. It takes me until he has picked me up and is pulling me away from the quickly growing pile of dead freak-a-zoids, that I realize I had fallen at some point during this attack. We turn the corner of the building and James puts me down and places his hands on the wall, using his body to shield my own.

My heart races as I turn my eyes up to his tight jaw line, and his dust covered hair. My eyes move along his muscular arms and, for some reason, I can feel myself blushing.

The ground stops shaking, and my hearing slowly improves to the point where I can hear Kota beside us panting loudly. I blink up at James. "What was that?"

"An ambush." James pushes himself off the wall and carefully peers around the corner to look at the bodies.

"On us?" I gasp slightly as I run my fingers through Kota's fur.

"Not on us, the freak-a-zoids. We just so happened to be in the wrong place at the wrong time."

"Did they not see us?"

"I don't know, Jemma. I haven't exactly had time to talk to them yet."

I take a quick drink of water, then follow him carefully down the street lined with the bodies and body parts of the freak-a-zoids.

I turn my attention to the damaged buildings as I try to figure out where this assault came from. I notice boards running along the roof and point up at them.

James nods his head. Drawing his gun, he motions to the steps of the fire escape belonging to one of the buildings.

Once on the roof, we see a small group of people sitting at a table talking quietly amongst themselves while drinking beer and laughing about their successful kills.

"That was a rude way to greet guests to New York by dropping bombs on them." James points his gun at one of them, ready if they decide to attack.

The people at the table quickly jump up, guns drawn on us.

I then pull my gun and point it at one of them as well.

Kota stands behind me growling loudly, baring his teeth.

"Did we scare you? Surely not as badly as we were when you tried to kill us." I glare at them, while watching them closely.

The people whisper among themselves before lowering their guns. "If we had known, we probably wouldn't have dropped them so closely to where you were."

"Maybe, you should have looked first." I retort as I slowly walk to the edge, look over and look back at them. "It is not that difficult."

James lowers his gun and gestures for me to do the same. I hesitate but eventually I, too, lower my gun.

"Sorry about that." One of the men seems sincere about his apology. "Welcome to New York. We are the Yankees, a group of settlers and mercenaries who have taken over New York's rooftops for a few years now."

I raise a brow slightly, looking to James who decides to speak for both of us. "I am James, Kota, our dog and this fireball here is Jemma."

"What brings you to New York?" the same settler questions.

"Just passing through, we are trying to make our way to Maine."

"What is in Maine?" they all choir at the same time.

James, who doesn't like the inquisitive people he does not know, simply mentions we are making our way there to make a settlement. "I like the ocean, and I am hoping Jemma will as well."

With little to no more questions, the Yankees show us the path over the rooftops and point in the direction we need to go to get to Vermont. Once they witness us climb down the set of fire escapes, they return to where we found them.

We keep quiet as we pick up speed, attempting to get into the next state before it gets too late at night.

We find a church resting in a grove of dead trees and decide it will be our place to rest for the night. The church is still and a chill works its way in through the holes in its roof. Even with a draft, this church is much safer than camping outside. With each new state we enter, new threats surround us, even if we cannot see them. They are still out there.

Once we are settled in, I curl up on the floor beside Kota and attempt to get a bit of rest. James places his sleeping bag by the door, so he will be able to guard it while he takes first watch. I close my eyes as I toss and turn, attempting to sleep that night, but I am anxious. I know we are almost there, our final stretch before we are in Maine, and our real mission is at hand as we try and find Eden.

Chapter 22

Maggie walks over to me with her usual overly cheerful smile covering her face.

"Hello there, what brings you to the Garden of the Gods?"

In realize in my dreams I can never hear my voice, but I always have some sort of response to whatever has been said in each of them.

"Oh, you look terrible, child. You look like a wet goose, you do." Maggie, as cheerful as always, wraps her arm around me as she walks me back to her hut. "You can stay with me tonight. I have a spare bed for friends." Maggie spends the whole night talking to me about the trip I am on, and reminding me about my trip to Maine to find Eden.

By the next day, I have set off again before the sun has fully risen in the sky.

Suddenly I'm in Chicago and am shocked as I hear about a man being tossed across a whole room.

I was growing tired, but I have to keep going.

I only stop when I see the bodies of all of the freak-a-zoids in New York.

I jolt awake, looking around quickly as I try to compose myself and get my bearings again. I blink as I look out one of the clear panes of the stained glass window of the church, clouds slowly drifting past it. In a way it reminds me of when Alise and I would stare at the clouds and guess what the shapes looked like. But that was long ago, before the war, and before I learned Lillian and Alise betrayed me.

James looks over to me, noticing I am looking out the window. "Can't sleep?" he questions.

"No." I let out a sigh. "I keep retracing my steps in coming here, but every time I meet someone, it is like they don't even know who I am. It does not make sense."

"Odd." James ponders the dream before changing subjects. "We are almost to Maine. After that, we just have to figure out which lighthouse the tunnel is under." His efforts to reassure me only make my anxiety worse.

"Yeah," I rub my eyes slowly as I take a deep breath.

The journey thus far has felt so exhausting, I often wonder if it happened at all. Perhaps all of this has just been a dream, especially considering I keep having recurring dreams that seem to keep taking me through all of the places I have already been.

After all of the death we have witnessed in the world, I hope Eden is real, so at least I can see what this world should be like. Then maybe, just maybe, we can take some of Eden and return the world to what it once was. But, that job is something we will have to take on after we find it.

We cut through New Hampshire which, in my opinion, feels like the quickest of all the states to get through. To be fair though, we stick so close to the edge of it, it takes no time at all before we have gone through the whole state.

It takes us a few days to get to Portland, Maine, but once we are there, James seems to have decided right away which lighthouse we should check first.

As ambitious as he is, though, we decide to rest in the city for the night. I want to object, but I am as tired as James and Kota are, and I know we need to rest.

We have a lot to do, and it is too late to do anything else tonight, so we will rest.

James picks up a map of Portland from a gift shop in the lobby of the hotel we decide to stay in for the night.

I walk into the gift shop and take a few lighthouse figures as well as a map for myself, so I don't always have to crane over James' shoulders to get an idea of what he is talking about. I rejoin James in the lobby, which is where we plan to set up camp for the night. As I walk past him at the table, I look over his shoulder at the map he has begun to study. Old habits are hard to break, I guess.

"We will try here first." He points to the map. "That lighthouse is called Portland's Headlight. It was built in 1791 and is one of the oldest lighthouses in all of Maine."

I raise a brow as I sit across from him. "Why do you think it will be there? Don't you think the reality of it is it should be in one of the newer ones?"

"Well for starters, it has a large house attached to it and secondly, I would be surprised if there wasn't some kind of hidden passage there somewhere. Especially since Maine was originally one of the locations for the Underground Railroad."

I shrug slightly. "It is worth a shot." I look down to my own map before getting up and walking over to the lobby couch, I curl up on its cushions and drift off to sleep. The nerves of the following day sends me back into my nightmares, making me wish I could stop dreaming these dreams. Just for one night.

I was gathering with the Yankees outside Portland and whispering something to them. They all nod and we split into two separate groups. I can see where James and I are sleeping, and instantly wake up, gasping for air.

I crawl over to where James is fast asleep and shake him slightly. He groans and shoves me away. I shove him hard in the arm and continue to shake him to wake him up.

"What?" He groans, half asleep.

"I just had a dream." I look around the room nervously.

"And? What makes this one different from the rest?" He barely opens his eyes.

"Something is outside," I whisper, shaking him hard again as he began to snore.

"You just said it was a dream, Jemma. A nightmare, I am sure." James groans as he turns over.

"James!" I shove him hard in his back.

"Go to sleep, Jemma. It was just a dream!" James snarls as he closes his eyes tightly.

As I am about to yell at him, shots begin to fire into the windows, breaking the glass.

James jumps up quickly, looking around for a moment before he leads us out the back entrance of the hotel.

"I told you!"

"Yeah," James takes out his gun. "Save your I told you so's until we get out of this mess, would you?"

We bust out the back door, only to find two of the Yankees are on either side, blocking our escape routes as if they knew we would take this way out of the hotel.

A soft voice comes from behind us. "I knew I would find you." The voice is shallow but sounds familiar. I turn to confront the person, but before I can look at their face, I am hit in the head and fall unconscious.

Chapter 23

When I finally come to, I am groggy and tied to a chair. Also, I am very certain this is not the result of me trying to get into one of the rooms on floor seven and eight at the Mart Settlement. I try to look around at the empty room I am in, and groan as I try to get my bearings while dealing with a splitting headache. What did they hit me with? A rock?

The door to the room opens as one of the Yankees I had met days before walks in. He turns to look out the door. "She is awake," he mentions to a person in the hall.

A voice responds from somewhere in the hall. "Good, get the equipment ready."

Whatever is going on has me wondering where James and Kota are being held, and all I know is I need to get out of here and rescue them. A few moments pass and the Yankee who had been in here returns and gives me some form of a shot which causes my vision to go blurry before I fall asleep again.

When I awake for the second time, I find myself strapped to a table that has a large light directly over my head, which makes looking around this room almost impossible.

"What is going on?" I can feel my words are slurring, most likely from the drug they gave me. My headache pounds, making my stomach feel uneasy, if I make sudden movements, I will likely throw up. I make a mental note and close my eyes.

"You will find out soon enough when everyone is ready," the guard's words, cryptic, clearly on strict orders to say nothing to me.

"I don't know if anyone has told you," I begin as I move my wrists trying to get free. "I hate surprises." I pull my hand hard towards my body, expecting the tight restraints to snap at the action alone. Instead, they do nothing, so I try a few more times getting annoyed at how strong these are.

"Your attempts to break out of those are pointless, ma'am." The guard sounds annoyed at me for even attempting it.

"Ma'am? Breaking out? What gave you the idea I was trying to break out?" I sigh, softly mumbling to myself. "Breaking out would only count if I am actually successful."

"I can see you trying to get loose from your cuffs from here. You won't be able to, those cuffs are made of some of the strongest metal on this whole planet." The guard sounds so proud of himself, as though he has created them with his bare hands.

"That can't be true," I struggle again slightly with the cuffs.

"What do you mean?" He sounds genuinely concerned about how he could possibly be wrong about something.

"Well, the cuffs can't be made of the hardest metal, because, you see the hardest metal is clearly clanking around in that big head of yours." I smile softly. The silence tells me I may have hurt this person's ego just a little bit.

"Stop talking to the prisoner," someone orders.

"Why? I was just beginning to have a little fun."

"You are not here to have fun."

"You could have fooled me and, not to be rude but, why can't the other guy talk to me when you can?" A smile flickers across my face.

The guard, now realizing they have just started a conversation with me lets out a loud sigh before going quiet. I softly begin to laugh and shake my head, only to stop suddenly once I recall that my head is still pounding, and I can feel that I am about to throw up.

I hear the door open to the room followed by the voice of a third person. "I warned you both not to talk to her, but did you listen? No. Now look at both of you, moping around with what exactly, damaged egos? Go guard something else, I can deal with her myself." I can hear the others leave slowly, leaving me alone with this new person.

"So, are you going to tell me what exactly is going on here?"

The person in here walks around the room picking up and moving things to a tray.

"Silent treatment." I sigh. "How dull."

"Do you really think your mind tricks will work on me?"

"Honestly? A little bit, yeah."

"Well, they won't. I've known you far too long to let your tricks get to me."

I sit there for a moment, trying to recall how I know their voice but this headache is making it impossible to place who they are. "All right, you win, I can't figure it out. Who are you?"

The person laughs. "Typical. Three months and you already forget what I sound like."

"That is a terrible hint. For all I know you could be the leader of the followers of the Glowing One or one of his followers." Even though the person said I could not get to them, my latest comment has caused them to slam the tray of tools down loudly by my head, letting me know I have struck a nerve. My head pounds as a response.

"Do you really think you can forget me that easily, Jemma?" With those words, the light above my head is turned off. I open my eyes slowly and blink in surprise as I see Alise staring down at me, fury in her bright blue eyes.

The image I try to hold onto about Alise is that she is pretty much perfect, her skin smooth, her eyes soft blue. She always kept her hair in a perfect bun on top of her head, and her clothing had no flaw on it at all or she would not wear it. This new Alise is far from the Alise I had known. This one, harsh and angry, her clothing caked in dirt and blood, and her hair loose at her shoulders. Her face covered in three long gashes that healed as best as they could and turned into permanent scars on her right cheek. The eye on the right side of her face looks milky and glossed over, meaning she must be blind in that one eye. I can't blame her for being mad, but she started all of this and I did what I thought was best at the time. She can't really blame me for all of that, can she?

"Alise? How are you?" I blink as I take in her new look.

"Alive?!" She shouts as she balls her hands into fists.

"I was going to say here but, if that is what you want me to ask, then that works too."

"You want to know why I am here? It is quite simple really; I am here because I need you." Alise turns and walks towards the door.

"Need me for what?"

"You will find out soon enough." With that, the room grows quiet as she leaves. I stare silently up at the ceiling as I try to figure out what Alise has planned for me. Whatever it is, it is not going to be good. I can already tell.

For the first time since everything happened, deep down, I am a little afraid of what might happen next. Alise has become unpredictable, meaning anything could happen, and not knowing terrifies me.

Chapter 24

At some point I believe they gave me some more of whatever drug they had previously given me, because when I woke up, I was struggling to remember what was going on. I know I am still strapped to the table, but now, there are a bunch of doctors in the room, whispering with excitement.

My head still hurts and my body is numb. I look around as best as I can, trying to take in everything before Alise begins to speak to the crowd of doctors.

"Gentlemen, thank you for making the trip out here for this glorious day in history." She smiles as she walks over to my side while they all clap loudly. My head pounds with each clap, and I groan slightly. "For those of you who do not know what reason I have for bringing you all here, it is quite simple. But first I would like to introduce you to my "twin," Jemma. Now, she is not actually my twin. My mother created her to be, what would you call this? She is my own personal living donor. If something in me dies or gets sick, she carries all of the exact things I need." Gasps come from the crowd. I blink at the way she describes me, remembering all of the times I protected her, all those times I loved her, and this is what I get in return. I know now that I should have done the job myself in Genesis. I can feel pain in my heart but I cannot understand this pain I am feeling. "Now, I need each and every one of you for a very special task. I personally chose all of you for all the specialties you have as doctors. From plastic surgery, to neurology to even cardio, you all will have a very big part in all of this. Some of you may wonder what you are all about to be a part of." I can almost feel her smile as she moves away from me, across the room and over to a board. "It is quite simple, you will all be helping me accomplish a complete human transplantation with a living donor to an awake recipient." The doctors gasp in awe, then begin to whisper among themselves before she adds. "I know, it will likely be a challenge. It is already an extremely difficult procedure, as well as time consuming. But, I have faith in all of your skills to successfully accomplish this. Plus I will die without this transplant, so I need all of your help."

Everyone begins to clap loudly, which does not help with my headache. While the cheers are louder than normal, I test the cuffs to see if I can break free of them, once more knowing I am quickly running out of time.

After a few moments, everyone leaves minus the two Yankees I had gotten the pleasure to meet earlier. I stare at the roof and begin to whistle a soft eerie tune, which, not to my surprise, makes both of my guards shift nervously.

"Stop whistling," one orders.

"Why, it is not like I am actually doing anything wrong."

"That whistling is irritating us." His words unconvincing.

I choose to ignore his request to stop whistling and continue, my eyes closed now as I play my eerie tune. I stop the moment the door opens. I turn to see the doctors all in run-down scrubs. Alise, in a long hospital gown, follows behind them, a big smile on her face.

"For this all to go as smoothly as possible during the procedure, I ask all doctors who are not currently a part of the first steps, to go get some rest. Don't you worry, there will be plenty for all of you to do when you return later."

Some of the doctors leave. I feel my eyes get blurry and I turn towards Alise. "You don't need to do this."

She walks over and looks down at me. "Of course I do. That little incident you pulled in Genesis is the reason this has to happen today."

"What do you mean?" I blink at her.

"Oh, Jemma, did you really think your little stunt would not have repercussions?" She let out a sigh as she shakes her head. "You cannot seriously think, after all this time, after all you have learned, that you would get away with it?" She scoffs slightly. "Please, you destroyed everyone and everything I loved and, because of that, every cell in you belongs to me. You were created to be my perfect donor, no matter what I need, whether it is a bone graft, kidney, anything at all, I can get them and I never have to wait for it. It is you who will help me live forever. You are my fountain of youth, so to speak. With your blood, I will never get sick again, and your skin will keep me looking young forever. Not to mention your bones and organs. I can become exactly what I was born to be, and everything Mother wanted for me. And you, you will be used for exactly what you were designed for and then discarded just like you tried to do to me and Mother in Genesis."

I blink in shock as I stare up at her. "Alise, you cannot be serious. You are not the type to take a life."

"Not the type? You are one to talk, Jemma. I didn't release a whole bunch of lab animals into an underground lab full of people, did I?" I look at her scar and she smiles slightly. "Exactly, you did that."

"Well, that was a mistake on my part.," I sigh as I shift slightly. "I should have thrown you in one of the cages with them, that way I would have known for a fact you were dead."

Alise, unenthused by my words, grabs a scalpel and holds it to my throat, her hand shaking as she glares at me in anger.

"Do it," I whisper. "As I see it right now, you still need me."

Alise stands over me a moment more before slamming the scalpel on the tray and walks over to her table.

"I knew you couldn't do it, as weak as you have always been."

"I am not weak. I just know I will take great pleasure in watching them remove each and every inch of skin off of you. I look forward to seeing every drop of blood be removed from you." I could feel the smile on her face, and the confidence she held tightly to.

"Well, I hate to tell you this, but you are going to be highly disappointed." I return my own smile now.

"Disappointed how exactly? You are stuck here, you are not going anywhere except to your grave."

"Didn't Lillian ever tell you not to judge a book by its cover?"

I felt her sit up slightly as she turns to me. "After what you did to my mother, you have no right to even bring her up, let alone say her name, Jemma. But that is also where you are wrong. I know every chapter of your book, and you have absolutely nothing you can hide from me. I also know how your book will end, it will be because of me." Triumphantly she lays back down on her table.

"That is where you are wrong, Alise." I begin to smile, the faces of the people who have become my friends on this journey, the new life I have made has done nothing but make me stronger. "There are so many more things about me now than you will ever know."

Alise must have nodded to the doctors to begin, because they start moving around and getting ready to start the procedures. I can hear her asking the doctor for something before speaking to me once more. "Well, Jemma, I hate to have to tell you this, but your journey is about to end."

I stare up at the ceiling. I know I should care about what is happening to me, but I don't. I think about all the people I have met, and the person I have become in such a short time and realize how much a person can change. My mind goes to Kota, the sweet, yet somewhat irritating, dog. Then to James, the irritating, yet sweet, soldier boy who somehow knocked down some of the walls to my heart whether I want to admit it or not.

I am content. If this is my day to die, I will be alright with it. I will regret not finding Eden, but I had tried and that is all that matters. I hope James and Kota will be alright, and I hope they will get out safely. It does not matter what happens to me. I chose this life. James and Kota may have joined me of their own free will. But I do wish I had not dragged them into this situation with Alise. They do not deserve this.

As the doctors hold up scalpels, the door to the room is bashed open. I quickly break free of my cuffs, as they have become weakened by my former attempts, and stand up on slightly numb, shaking legs. I focus my sights on Alise's terrified face.

This will end today. The final showdown between Alise and myself is about to begin.

Chapter 25

As the door to the room slams open, I jump off the surgical table. Grinning instantly the moment I see James and Kota, looking a little worse for wear but here.

"What took you so long?" I smile as I look to some of the doctors who immediately drop their scalpels and run out of the room.

"We got a little tied up." James smiles as he sends two of the Yankee guards running.

"Yeah, I know what you mean." I nod my head to the surgical table.

Alise slowly gets off the table, looking between James and me, fear covering her features.

"What is this here? Alise?" James blinks in shock as he looks as if he has seen a ghost.

She does not respond, just looks around the quickly emptying room.

"No one is going to protect you, Alise." James watches her as he moves slightly to block the door.

Alise, a cornered rat with a fight or flight look runs for the secondary door, but it is locked. She pulls frantically on the door, breathing heavily as she keeps tugging.

"When you first mentioned all I am to you is a live donor, I thought about killing you." She turns to look at me, panic covering her facial expression. "But, instead." I turn to James, a gentle smile forming on my face. "I am choosing to do something I didn't know was an option before, something my former self wouldn't have done. I am going to walk away. Your blood will not be on my hands. I have already killed far too many innocent people. I will not add you to that list."

James smiles as he lowers his weapon, Kota, beside him, pants happily.

I smile and slowly walk towards them and away from Alise.

"What? You can't just walk away, Jemma!"

"Are you ready to go?" James looks down at me, a smile comes to my face as I look into his welcoming eyes.

"I am ready." James leads the way out and I slowly follow after him and Kota. Alise runs after me, raising the scalpel in hand. She brings it down as she begins to attack me.

As swiftly as I had been with Mark, I grab her hand with the scalpel in it and turn it on her before she has a chance to notice what is going on. Shock covers her face as she staggers back away from me, blood pooling from under her hospital gown, tears coming to her eyes, reminding me of the young girl I once knew.

I watch as Alise falls to the ground holding her side tightly, tears falling from her eyes. "Help me." She begs as she coughs up some blood.

I feel torn, do I save her? Or do I leave? All my life, all I wanted to do was to find her. I wanted to save her, but all I ever was to her was expendable. I turn away from her and begin to make my way to the door. I can hear her calling after me.

"Jemma! You can't just leave me here to die. You are programed to save me, get back here and help me!"

I slowly turn to look at her. I can see the hope in her eyes. "The thing you don't seem to realize about programing is it can be changed. All of my life, I have been designed to save you, but there are some things even I cannot save you from." I turn and make my way out the door.

"Jemma." James slowly follows after me, Kota on his heel.

I turn to look at him, and I could feel wetness on my face. Am I crying?

James softly runs his thumb across my cheek, wiping off a tear. I lean into his hand as I look up at him. "Are you alright?" His voice is soft.

"I am fine," I whisper gently. I lead us over to the shore where I stare for a long while at the water as it softly hits the rocks. It makes me think of simpler times. I feel calm here. If we never find Eden, I think I will want to come back here and live. Away from the big cities and away from all of the memories.

James is standing behind me, also looking out at the sea quietly.

I turn to him. "Did I make the right choice leaving her like that?"

He thought of his words carefully before looking down to me. "I feel you did what you thought was best." He could see the sadness in my eyes as he slowly placed his hand on my shoulder. "But, in saying that, not killing Alise, even after everything you have been put through, takes a vast amount of strength, strength I honestly don't know if I would have if it had been me in your place. You have grown so much since the days you were in Fort Exodus, and I believe Aaron would have been proud of you."

I let out a slight sigh, the feel of him awkwardly placing his hand on my shoulder is strange and uncomfortable. I stand still while looking out at the sea. I can feel myself wanting to push his hand away, to remain safe in the bubble I have create for myself but, at the exact same time, I longed for more of whatever this feeling is that he has given me.

I know James is right. I did make the choice I was meant to but, at the same time, could I have been more merciful? Should I have saved her or killed her? Allowing her to finally have peace once again like she had the day she walked into the lab moments before she saw me.

James removes his hand and heads up to the house on the rocks. I slowly follow after him where we find a place and settle in for the night. Kota curls up beside me and I find for the first time, in a very long time, I sleep straight through with no glimpse of nightmares. The connection I had with Alise has been severed. I am free, whether I am ready to accept it or not.

Chapter 26

I get up early the next day, even before James. I take Kota outside. To my surprise, overnight it has snowed. I shrug my jacket on and pull the faux fur hood over my head to keep my ears warm. I watch as Kota runs around excitedly, hopping into piles of snow.

As Kota has the time of his life, I turn my attention to the snow covered rocks the water continues to brush up against. I shiver slightly as I see my breath. It is cold, and the cool air coming off the water only seems to lower the temperature more. I run inside long enough to grab a broken chair so I can sit and watch the sunrise.

The way the sky looks when the sun rises has to be one of my most favorite sights. The colors of pink, blue and orange as they take over the once dark skies give promise of a brand new day where anything can happen.

I am so deep in thought, I do not hear James leave the house, or hear him walk over to me, not until I can feel something on my shoulders and it snaps me back to reality.

"Couldn't sleep?" James questions as he stares off at the sun rise.

"I slept better than most days, but it was not a very long rest." I pull the blanket around my shoulders and cocoon myself where I sit.

"Same here." He let out a gentle sigh.

"It is peaceful here."

"Yes, it is. Maybe once all of this is over, I will come back here to stay. I feel like I have been in the army for most of my life. I want to retire, and here is exactly where I would want to retire to."

I turn to look at him. "Won't that mean you have to go back to Fort Exodus to see if that dream of yours to retire is even possible?"

He lets out a soft sigh as he smiles. "Most likely, yes. But the trip there to see if I can retire is worth it. Even if it is not soon, the thought of retiring will make the years left in service far easier to manage."

I smile and stand up. "I am going to go grab some food before we go hunting for Eden." I make my way carefully though the snow and back towards the house. James must have started a fire before coming out, the flickering of light comes from its windows promisingly. I can hear James crunching though the snow as he follows behind me, but the crunching stops.

"Jemma?" James' voice seems more confused than normal, and I turn to look at him. He is holding a piece of paper and studying it with a stern facial expression.

"What is it?" I slowly work my way back over to him.

"Look at this. This can't be a coincidence."

I raise a brow curiously as he hands me the paper he was holding. I look at it, confused as to what I was being shown, then I realize it is the pamphlet about the Portland Headlight Lighthouse. I want to ask James why he is looking at it with such determination, but all he does is point behind me. I turn to look once more, and that is when I see it. We had been staying in the exact building that is in the article. I gasp as I turn from the pamphlet to the house and back down. We have been at the Portland Headlight Lighthouse this whole time and had not been the wiser.

"Nothing is coincidence," I whisper softly.

The fact that we stayed the night in the lighthouse we were searching for gives us new found hope. We eat hastily as we have so much to do now that we are here. I almost did not even want to eat but was forced to with words saying *just because we found it does not mean you should not eat and keep up your strength.*

We decide we will search both the house and the lighthouse in hopes there is a passageway here somewhere that will lead us to Eden.

We split up, I take the lighthouse, while James looks through the house. The house is connected to the lighthouse, so I just make a walk through the attached part of the building. At the door that should lead into the lighthouse, I see a padlock which keeps the door tightly shut. Using the end handle of my gun, I slam down hard on the lock and it quickly breaks open. Slowly opening the door, I can instantly smell the mustiness of this place. I make my way up the twisted metal stairs until I come across a group of broken ones which sends me back down the way I had originally come, knowing there is no way for me to get any father up even if I tried.

Back on the main floor, I stare up at the spiral stairs, knowing a secret tunnel will not be all the way at the top of the lighthouse. I turn my attention to the ground, in hopes of finding a trap door. Moving debris as I go, my heart races as I try to put together that I have just found a trap door.

With a deep breath, I open the door, which creaks loudly. It reveals a dark hole and a ladder leading into it. Grabbing my flashlight, I shine inside the hole. It looks like a cellar but until I go down, I won't know for sure if that is all that is down there. As I am about to go down into the cellar, James comes into the lighthouse.

"Did you find anything?" James and Kota make their way over to where I am by the cellar's entrance.

"I am not sure. Did you find anything?" I turn my attention from the dark hole in the ground up to his face curiously.

"Nope, the house has nothing of interest."

"Then I suppose this hole that leads to the cellar is our only shot of finding a possible passageway here at Portland's Headlight."

I quickly climb down the steps, followed by James who again has to carry Kota down because he doesn't want to wait for us on the main floor. We turn our flashlights on and slowly search. There is not much down here except a few empty boxes. I let out a sigh of disappointment as we look over every corner.

"We tried." James couldn't hide the disappointment in his voice, especially when I feel the same.

"Maybe it will be in the next one." I turn to look at him, and offer some sort of fake reassurance.

"Maybe. You first." James points his flashlight to the ladder.

I begin to make my way back up the ladder when I hear a slight click noise behind me. I freeze. "What was that?" I could feel my body's defenses kick in, the desire for fight or flight rushing around in my head.

"I don't know, let me check it out. Don't move." James and his flashlight disappear for a moment before I hear him speak again. "Jemma, you won't believe this. Come over here and look what Kota found."

I make my way back down and move to where I see James' flashlight. He is petting Kota on the head and has a big grin on his face. "What did he find?" I question. James steps on a stone on the ground and it reveals a secret panel on the wall pop open slightly. I stare at it in shock, before turning from James down to Kota. "I can't believe it."

"Better believe it, Jemma. Nothing is coincidence."

I grin as I move over to the panel and force it open. With my flashlight, I shine it in the area the panel reveals and notice it is a long tunnel carved into the stone, leading even deeper into the darkness. I turn and look to James and smile before opening it wide to give room for him to see as well. We both turn to look down the tunnel. This is it, all or nothing is waiting for us in this tunnel.

Chapter 27

The deeper in the tunnel we go, the louder our footsteps echo around us. Kota is panting behind me, and I force out a soft, even breath as I begin to notice the walls are starting to get closer together and the roof is getting lower. We crouch to make our way through one long section because the roof is so much lower than most other spots, which takes James a bit of extra time since he is much taller.

We stop as we come to a large area that is an open room, with three tunnels leading off. I blink as I look to the tunnels.

"Which path do we take?"

James, who is as lost as I am on what path to choose, stares for a moment.

Kota pushes his way past us and runs directly towards the farthest path on the left.

"I guess we will try that one." James grins as we follow Kota. He did help us find this cave in the first place. What is the worst that can happen?

We keep all conversations quiet as we work our way down this path Kota chose. The air in this tunnel is beginning to feel wet and the walls are damp. We only stop when we find ourselves beside an underground lake. The water sparkles as we run our flashlights over its surface. We can also see the reflections of the stalactites from above the water. I turn my attention to the rock formations in the ceiling of the cave then back down to the water.

James must have seen my facial expression because he smiles at me. "Beautiful down here, isn't it?"

I feel my cheeks redden as I nod slightly.

We continue forward as we follow the water through a tunnel and into another, which declines slightly at first then a lot more. We have to move slowly, with the ground wet as well as the walls, we do our best to keep from slipping.

At the bottom of the inclined tunnel, we enter a large room where more carved stones lead us to a very large carved door.

My heart races as we make our way over to the door. I have to fight my mind and not let my hopes get up too high as I move my flashlight across the door curiously, knowing, thanks to Kota, there has to be a trigger for it in here somewhere.

James and I both look around the room quickly, moving, and stepping on every stone we can find. Nothing is working. I let out a loud sigh as I have begun to feel defeated. We lost. I sit on a boulder by me and a crack noise comes from the door.

James quickly runs over and slides the door open before I get off the boulder, he peers inside the door before turning back to me. "Jemma, come see this."

Getting up from the boulder quickly, I make my way over to the door, my jaw instantly drops. Inside this door is a large hallway that looks to be made out of some sort of Plexiglas. As we move farther in to the room, I scan my flashlight across the walls until I spot a door, also made of Plexiglas. I turn to James, who nods his head slowly.

"Here goes nothing." I hold my breath as I try to open the door.

A light instantly comes on, blinding both James and myself for a moment. Blinking, we enter another long hallway made out of the same metallic material as the door. This long hallway leads us to another door similar to the one we first saw as we entered into the cave. This door though, has no handle on it, leaving us curious as to how we are supposed to open it.

Once all of us enter this hallway, the door behind us quickly slams shut and an alarm begins to blare loudly, the bright lights turn yellow. We run back to the door we entered and try the handle but it is locked. We are trapped.

A voice recording comes on. "Decontamination process to begin in five, four, three-"

Something along the walls begins to rise from the floor to the ceiling.

"-two, one."

The thing that had just raised up above us suddenly begins to spray us with water from our heads first down to our feet. Once it reaches the floor, it disappears and the voice returns once more. "Decontamination process complete." The door ahead of us unlocks with a click.

James and I turn to each other, then to a very unhappy Kota. We timidly make our way to the door and find ourselves entering an identical tunnel with the same door on the far side of it.

"After all of that, they can't even dry us off with air of some sort?" I mumble, stepping through the door to this hallway.

Another alarm goes off, both doors lock again and the prerecorded voice returns "Dry off zone commencing in five, four-"

"You had to say something, didn't you, Jemma." James looks annoyed as he looks down at me.

"-Three, two, one." Large fans above our heads begin to blow air on us and lasts at least five minutes. They are so loud we can't even hear ourselves think. After five minutes the fans turn off and the voice returns. "Dry off complete." The door ahead of us clicks and unlocks.

I turn to James who, in my opinion, looks more terrified than I am, and Kota whimpers, not wanting to come across any more surprises. I take a deep breath and lead the way into yet another hallway. This is all beginning to make me feel nervous. Our senses heightened as we look around the tunnel suspiciously. On the far end of the tunnel is another door and to one side a large red button sits on a long metal pipe.

"Should I push the button?" I stare at it, knowing nothing good ever comes from hitting a big red button.

James sighs softly beside me. "Might as well."

I nod, taking a deep breath as I press the big red button. Silence fills the room and I turn to James who shrugs slightly when nothing happens.

As we are about to give up, a voice comes from behind me. "Welcome!" I turn to see a hologram of a tall lady in a white dress, her hair dark red and down to her shoulders. The glass on either side of us tinted and turned black, the lights above us turn off as well. "Throughout history, man has set to destroy the world." Pictures begin to play on the walls. "Man will never change, no matter who is in control. Leaders promise to end the wars that threaten to destroy everything, wars they created, but they, too, were driven by only one thing; greed. The world, as it always does, fell into chaos and when all hope was about to be lost forever, a group took it upon themselves to save it. They took seeds of all plants and trees, they captured animals to protect them in case there ever was nuclear destruction. The plants and seeds they took could be used to help rebuild if anything were to happen to the world above. To no surprise, the bombs did fall and left destruction in their wake, destroying and changing the whole world forever." The pictures change to the world as it is now. "But all hope was not lost, for the place the founders made still exists; an Eden among a world of waste." The lights quickly come back on, causing James and myself to blink a few times. The door ahead of us unlocks and opens slightly. We instantly hear something we have not heard in years; birds. "Welcome to Eden." The door fully opens, revealing a large, lush forest as far as the eye could see. Flowers covering the ground in every color you could imagine, and songs from birds I had almost completely forgotten.

James and I stare in awe, Kota stands beside us and sniffs the air as he wags his tail.

"I can't believe this place actually exists." James gasps.

"You better believe it," I whisper with a big smile covering my face.

Chapter 28

Eden, an oasis so deep in the ground, if one had not been looking for it would have never even known of its existence. Full of every type of plant and animal you could see. Temperature controlled rooms connected to the main one, gives the animals and all other living things a chance to thrive in the climate they were meant to be in.

In the center of the main area, high above all of the rest, stands a large oak tree. By the size of it, it had to be a few hundred years old, leaving us to wonder how long had Eden been around? As well as how did they know this was going to happen to the world above? I suppose with human's predictability, they must have always known this sort of chaos was going to take place at one point or another.

Birds fly around the area, chirping joyfully, appearing to not have even noticed we entered here. The animals, more curious, came over and sniffed at us, trying to understand the new invaders in their home.

We spend hours searching Eden and all it has to offer. Whoever created this place took great care to get each and every ecosystem as accurate as it would be above ground. By the way everything flourished, they had to have done a lot of research.

"It is so beautiful here." We walked deeper into Eden and came across a rose bush.

"Yes, it is."

"Imagine if everyone knew about this place." I lean over and carefully smell the flower.

"That is a very bad idea." James' words turn my attention to him curiously.

"Why do you say that?" I question. "Would they not all be happy?"

"Oh, they would be very happy, for about a minute before greed set in. Everyone would end up wanting Eden for themselves and, in the end, it would destroy all of this. I don't know about you, but with all the work the founders took to create this place, I don't want to be the reason it gets destroyed. For the safety of it, I wouldn't tell anyone who you don't fully trust. It will be better this way."

"If we cannot bring the world down to Eden, can we bring it up to them without them knowing where it came from?"

"It is hard to say for sure, but we could always take some seeds and plant them in random places, see if they will grow." He stays quiet for a moment then smiles. "You know what? That is actually a really good idea. Let's make it our goal to try and restore the world, one seed at a time."

"That sounds like a challenge worth facing to me." I offer him a smile before turning to look at Eden. Something large flies over my head and I quickly duck down. Afraid it is some sort of gigantic beast, I turn to see a small barn owl staring down at me with its big yellow eyes. After my heart stops racing, I turn my attention back to James. "I think I would like to set up and use the lighthouse as a permanent home, maybe even if it is just to protect Eden." I have nothing left for me in Colorado, and I want a place to finally have as my own. That way, even if I decide to travel a little, I will always have somewhere to return to.

"You will need help to do all of that, perhaps I can help you set it up. The seeds cannot be planted until spring, leaving quite a bit of time to wait."

I offer him a soft smile. "I can handle this. You still technically have the army to report to and, if it worries you too much that I will get in trouble, you have nothing to fear. This place will keep me busy for quite some time."

He let out a slight sigh. "You do have a good point. I will help you with all of this after I come back from my trip to Colorado."

After a bit more time in Eden, we decide to head back to the surface. Kota, even more reluctant to leave than we were. In the end with a little coaxing, Kota lead us back up the path to the surface. I couldn't blame him for wanting to stay. I wanted to stay too. But Eden, as much as we wanted it to be, was not our home, and we could not use it as such. It needed to remain as untampered with as possible. A few minutes was fine, but long times would allow the animals to get too comfortable with us. For their safety, we could not allow that to happen.

Once back on the surface, we close the hidden door and go back up the ladder to the lighthouse. We close the door to the lighthouse and go through the door that leads into the house. We sit at the table and look over the map James has.

"With spring still a ways away, we will have plenty of time to decide where we should first start planting seeds. We do not want it too close to here, for fear it will give away where Eden is."

I look at the map and ponder for a moment before pointing at a state. "What about New Hampshire? Near that church we stayed in."

"That should work just fine." James smiles. As he is about to say something else, his radio goes off and he rushes off to talk on it. He does that every time they call him. I am not mad, I understand some conversations could and probably should be confidential. "When? Alright I will leave in the morning." He reenters the room.

"Is everything alright?" I eye him curiously as he sits across from me.

"They want me to go back to Fort Exodus as soon as possible. Something has come up."

I smile and nod. I can tell he doesn't exactly trust the idea of leaving me alone, but I am twenty years old now and even I have noticed how much I have changed since the day I left Fort Exodus. "I will be just fine. Go."

He nods and gets back up from the table to pack.

I turn to Kota and run my fingers through his fur. "Looks like it is going to be just you and me for a while, the dynamic duo once again."

Kota pants as he wags his tail, causing me to smile. I could not help but imagine the day he came begging for food in the diner, the first day I was free from Fort Exodus. I had no clue how much I would value this partnership but now, I could not imagine not having Kota with me.

Chapter 29

In the morning, James spent a bit of time going around Portland, in hopes of finding a vehicle to get him to Colorado faster. Once he finds one to hopefully get him most of the way, he picks up his backpack and throws it into the passenger's seat and turns to me.

I hand him a couple of cans of food with a soft smile. As he takes them, his rough hand lingers a little longer against mine as he looks at me. I feel butterflies in my stomach from his lingering touch which causes me to pull my hand away quickly.

He looks at me a moment more before jumping into the driver's seat and turns on the car. "Don't go getting yourself into trouble while I am gone." He smiles that large smile I have grown to quite enjoy. "We both know how good you are at not following orders, especially when they come from me, but at least attempt to not get yourself killed before I return."

I let out a soft laugh. "I will try my best, but you know I am not promising anything."

He laughs loudly, throwing his head back as he does so. Once the laughing stops, he puts the car in drive and waves out the window at me.

I stand still, watching as he drives away. I would not be surprised if he was looking at me get smaller in his rearview mirror, both of us too stubborn to admit we are actually going to miss each other, especially now. I relish the thought of all the times I was thinking that James was a stuck-up army brat who followed orders and forced me to leave my family. But in the end, it turned out that even if he was a stuck-up army brat, he still had a good heart, which always says a lot about someone in this crazy world. My mind flashes back as I recalled his hand on my shoulder after what happened with Alise. I can feel my heart race and my cheeks turn red at the thought of his comfort, slightly wishing it had not ended. *What is this I am feeling for*

James? I question as I turn my attention from the road James was on, and went back into the house.

~ ~ ~

With James away for however long the army is going to keep him, I knew I would have plenty of things to do to keep my days busy.

I leave my house one day to head into Portland for supplies. I know there are many repairs that need done on the house to help turn it into a place I can call my own. I also know I will need to fix up the lighthouse. I make a mental note about wanting to find fresh water, if that is even possible, without taking from the lake underground near Eden.

On my adventures, I find a truck with just enough gas that I can fill it with any and all supplies and take them back to the house without having to make too many trips. I fill the truck's bed with any and all materials I can think of, from fences, to wood, as well as tools and anything else I might need.

As I make my second trip to pick up curtains, bedding and other such items, I freeze as I see a few of the Yankees wondering Portland. But they were on their way out of town and on their way back to New York. They were not liking the small town and felt they were better off back in their hometown, which they had fought so hard to protect.

The doctors who had come from Chicago, left and went back. Not wanting to taint their reputations, they kept all events that had gone down in Portland a secret.

Alise's body disappeared over night. I guessed one of the Yankees or one of the doctors decided to bury her. The ground is a little hard for that, but I didn't question their motives. They are free to do whatever they want.

With all of them gone, I am alone in Portland, minus a few freak-a-zoids here and there and, of course, my partner in crime, Kota, who enjoys running around Portland with me.

I take one final trip into town and find a few small gardening fences which, I figured, once we begin to plant these seeds they will need protected somehow and with a small fence around it, should give it the protection it needs to grow.

I drive the truck up beside the house and cover the small fence with a tarp, all wood and miscellaneous items are in whichever building they need to be in. That way, I do not have to drag them from one area to another.

The first nice day I have, I fix the roof of the house. Having no clue what I am doing, it did take a little longer than I expected. But, in my opinion, it did not look too bad after I was finished with it. It will keep the inside of the house dry and that is what matters most.

Months pass and the house and the lighthouse are slowly coming together. The stairs to the top of the lighthouse are now functional and the view from the top, absolutely breathtaking. I find myself going up there constantly to look out at the sea or over Portland. I look to see if anyone or anything has made its way into the city. All is still clear and I smile, content with this.

I can feel myself wishing for James to return, as content as I am with my freedom and proving to myself I can do anything I want on my own. I know I miss him, and it is absolutely aggravating to feel this way. What annoys me more though, I miss that feeling I felt that one day he had his hand on me. To feel his touch, and to miss it, irritates me. I am strong, and I can do anything I set my mind to and have proven to myself I can and will survive on my own. I have proven to myself I don't need him, but my heart, as cold as it is, wants to need him, wants to be protected by him. And deep down, that scares the shit out of me.

Iron Heart

Spring finally comes and all repairs are made to the house and lighthouse. I still have not heard from James and I am coming to accept I may not see him again. So, I go to Eden and take an acorn from the ground by the tree. This week I will go to New Hampshire and plant it like we had planned. It may take some time for it to grow, but it will be a good start. Before I leave, I lock the door to the house, hop into the truck, Kota by my side and we drive to the church so I can plant the seed.

I decide as we return to Portland, I will return in a month to check on how it is doing. A month should give it plenty of time to grow, I hope.

~ ~ ~

A month passes and it feels so much longer. The interior of the house is all set up. I have curtains up in every room as well as beds in three bedrooms. I repaired the couch and even fixed the table that was wobbling slightly. In the end, after everything was fixed, I was looking for anything to fix, whether it needed it or not. Perhaps the rooms could use painting.

Kota and I get into the truck and make our way to New Hampshire, to the church.

I can feel my heart race as we slow in front of it, my thoughts constantly questioning *what if this did not work. What if the oak tree isn't growing?* I take a deep breath and get out of the truck, Kota right behind me.

We walk around the church and a smile immediately comes to my face. Not too far off I can see a few shoots coming out of the ground. I run over to get a closer look. It worked. It will take quite some time for this to grow but the tree is growing.

Kota and I make our way quickly back to Portland and down into Eden. From our travels, I know some things will grow, whether it is a few various vegetables I had seen in the Garden of the Gods, or the underground ones that have been grown in Chicago at The Mart. But with this knowledge, we won't have to keep plants in the basements to have them grow. The ground is viable, and cannot only support an oak tree, but any and possibly everything Eden has to offer.

The thought of bringing this world back to how it once was gives me hope, and I long to share all this knowledge. I collect some seeds quickly from any and everything before making my way back up to the surface.

My smile fades as I see a strange vehicle sitting by the house. I slowly pull out my gun as I leave the lighthouse through the door to the house, slowly watching my step.

I notice the car is empty and the door to the house is open. I pull the hammer back on the gun and point it into the house. Kota's ears drop and his tail is tucked between his hind legs. Whoever is here, he didn't recognize.

"I do not know who you are, but you are in my home and I recommend if you want to live, you will show yourself."

Chapter 30

"Jemma?" a voice comes from the far side of the house.

I focus on the door to the living room, my gun pointed at it. The voice is familiar. "James?" His name rolls off of my tongue.

I see his face first, with that alluring smile that draws me in instantly. He is in normal clothing, cities, as he would call them. His hair, longer than before, is styled with some sort of hair gel.

My heart skips a beat as I beam. "James!" Before I can control my own emotions, I run up to him and wrap my arms around him tightly. He seems shocked at first but soon has me in his gentle and warm embrace. I look up into his dark green eyes, he seems so much taller than I remember him being. I can feel my heart race as he slowly moves the hair from my face, his hand lingering on my cheek as he leans down. I remember seeing movies when I was younger about what humans looked like when they kissed, but I had no idea this would be how it would feel. The anticipation, the desire to know how it feels, the fear of not being good enough crosses my mind in flashes.

All those thoughts erase the moment I hear someone behind him. "Ahem," the voice also familiar, echoes through the silence.

"Happy Birthday, Jemma." He whispers in my ear as he straightens up and lowers his hand from my cheek.

I blink slightly as I raise my brow to him, I try to get my voice back. "I do not know who you have been talking to, but my birthday is not for a few months."

He grins as he moves out of the way, revealing the door outside that was empty, only it is not empty anymore. I gasp instantly and quickly walk over to the door. "Bex!"

"Why, hello there, stranger." Bex is beaming brightly to me as she hugs me tightly. "James told me some of the adventures you have been on since I helped you escape Fort Exodus. Good job! And completely bad ass. I am sorry to hear about Alise though. With all the stories you had told me about her and your mother, it is a shock they could do that to you."

"It was a shock to me as well, believe me. I would have tried to get you out of Fort Exodus sooner, after the incident in Genesis though, I did ask James to see if he could bring you to me." I turn to James who is busy reuniting with Kota.

"It is not his fault. After the day I helped with your escape, I was approached by a group and have been working for them."

"What sort of group?" I question curiously.

"Are you planning to let her in?" James spoke up for the first time since the almost kiss, as he walks over to the couch followed by Kota.

As James goes to the couch, Bex watches him curiously before turning her attention back to me. "So, James huh?' Her smile large and as mischievous as always.

I can feel my face turn different shades of red. I toy with my hair as I turn away. "I don't know what you are talking about."

"Please, I am not blind. Are you going to tell me what that all was about? I thought we didn't like him." Bex pulls me out of the house and closes the door so we can talk without James listening in.

"He is not that bad." I admit quietly as I stare out at some of the buildings in Portland.

Bex snorts and stands in front of me to look me in the eyes. "If this is some sort of Stockholm syndrome, I can kick his ass for you."

I laugh loudly as I shove her slightly to the side. "If anyone has Stockholm syndrome, it is him. How else can you explain him liking a humanoid like me?"

"That is a fair point." Bex grins a wide smile again as she begins to laugh.

"Hey!"

We laugh as we enter the house. James looks up from the couch where he and Kota seem to be contently sitting. "Did you catch her up on all of your events since you left Fort Exodus?"

"Not quite, I will fill her in more later. So, what was it you were saying about this group who approached you?" I turn back to Bex who is also sitting on the couch now beside Kota.

"There is not a whole lot to say about them. They came to Fort Exodus and gave us a scenario to try and solve, the others from our class and myself. Turns out I had an idea they liked and I began working for them almost instantly."

"That is amazing, I knew you were smart. I am glad others can see that as well." I turn my attention over to a dozing James.

Bex grins brightly as she looks around the room while I start a fire in the fireplace. "Did you fix all of this by yourself?"

"Yes, I did. What can I say, I was left alone for a few months. I got bored."

"It looks great."

"Thank you."

James began to snore and I cannot help but laugh softly. I gently shake his shoulder. "I am awake." He groans.

I roll my eyes. "You have never been good at lying."

"I am not, I am awake. Tell me something you have done while I was gone."

I ponder slightly. "I went back to that church in New Hampshire."

He sits up and looks to me. "And?"

I smile softly to him. "And I think it will work. I have already seen progress."

"Progress for what?" Bex looks between us curiously.

James claps his hands happily with the news. "That is great." He gets up from the couch and stretches slightly. "We will show you tomorrow. Not to be rude but where can I get some sleep? The drive from Colorado to here has been exhausting."

Bex let out a gentle sigh at the thought of having to wait until morning to see this secret James and I have.

"It will be worth the wait, Bex. I promise." I smile at her before leading James to one of the spare bedrooms in the back of the house.

He inspects the room and, once pleased with it, bids us goodnight.

I show Bex to her room, which is across from James'. She puts her backpack in her room and meets me back in the living room, where we swap stories of what all we have been up to. Bex had finished her last job with the company she was working under around the time

James returned to Fort Exodus and, when he asked if she would like to join him on a trip back to Maine, she jumped at the opportunity. Only being given permission by the group she worked under that, if she found any useful technology, to bring it back to them. It was a fair trade; if she actually found anything she would never tell them.

I tell her about Alise and Lillian, and my side of what all happened between Fort Exodus and here. I could see the concern on her face as I tell her about my decision here in Portland, and letting Alise die with no help from me.

After I finish talking, she speaks up. "I think I have to agree with James. From how you were when you left Fort Exodus to this point, you have grown so much, into a person anyone should and would be proud of. You are like a whole new person. I know I am proud of you and your growth."

I smile. "I am proud of you too, Bex. You have accomplished a lot in such a short time."

Sleep finally began to catch up to us and Bex yawns slightly. I watch her walk to her room as I make my way to my room. "Hey Bex?"

"Yes?" She turns to me, a smile on her face.

"Welcome home."

"Thanks, you did a great job."

"Thank you. I will see you in the morning."

"Yes, you will."

We close our doors to our bedrooms, while Kota sleeps on the floor by the fire happily.

We have a big day ahead of us tomorrow, and I cannot help but look forward to it. Other than James, Kota and myself, no one has seen Eden. After tomorrow, Bex will as well. It is something exciting I can't wait to share with her.

Chapter 31

Morning feels like it came early. I had trouble sleeping which meant I am up long before the others. I make some food for breakfast and leave it for them once they wake up.

James, the second person to get up, is dressed in a tight black t-shirt and dark jeans. I look him over and smile softly.

"Cities look good on you." I admit as I blush slightly.

He looks over at me and smiles. "Jemma," he begins as he walks closer to me. "I want to apologize for my behavior yesterday. I should not have tried to kiss you."

I raise a brow and my heart races slightly. "Why would it be something to apologize for?"

He runs his hand through his hair as he turns away, not finishing the sentence.

"Is it me?" I whisper. "Is it because I am a humanoid?"

He turns to me and begins to laugh loudly. "Of course it is not you, Jemma. I figured it was me. I am this asshole who took you from your family, and then tried to keep you in Fort Exodus. So, if anything, it is me."

"That was a long time ago. Things change, people change. Don't get me wrong though. You are still an asshole, but you are also sweet, and have been here for me through every struggle I faced on this journey. I don't know if I could have done any of this without you."

"I know for a fact that is a lie, you, now and always, will be a strong independent woman who doesn't need anyone or anything. Because you show every day you can accomplish anything you put your mind to, and you don't need anyone else to help you with that."

I smile softly. "Even if that is true, I don't want to not need anyone or anything anymore. Those months you were gone, you were all I thought about when I was not fixing the house and lighthouse. It is silly, sappy and a little embarrassing, but it is true."

He laughs as he wraps his arms around me. "And you were all I thought of. I will not tell you how recklessly I drove to get back here to you sooner."

"I will. Would you two just kiss already? You still have that surprise to show me." Bex is leaning on the door frame of her room as she looks at us, a big grin on her face.

My mouth drops as I shove James away and Bex begins to laugh loudly. I huff. "Way to kill it, Bex. For that, eat and then we will talk about what we have to show you."

James grins as he makes his way to the table and sits down, slowly eating his food. Bex does the same and I feed Kota. Once they are done, we make our way through the house and into the lighthouse before going into the cellar.

"Is this what you are trying to surprise me with? A cellar?" Bex could not hide the disappointment in her voice. "Oh God, are you going to kill me and hide me down here?"

I shake my head and roll my eyes as James steps on the stone that opens the hidden door. Bex goes quiet, no longer panicking or asking questions. We take the tunnel down until we come to the three passages once more, and take the far left tunnel, past the underground lake and down the slope to the door. I press on the boulder and the door pops open.

I gesture for Bex to enter first, and all of us, except Kota, join her. He decides to stay outside this time. I can't honestly blame him.

Once we are all inside, the alarm goes off. James pulls me close as we watch Bex's face turn from calm to panic. She looks as afraid as we were the first time we came in here. I gently laugh as we all get soaked in the decontamination spray. Once it ends, she glares at me, looking like an angry wet cat. Her black hair sticking tightly to her back.

"What was that for?" She furiously asks as we make our way into the second chamber.

Before we can respond we are dried off, and have moved on to the next room with the single button on the pipe.

"Go ahead and press the button." I nod over to where it is, a smile on my face.

"Nothing is going to kill me, is it?"

"Nope, just push the button."

When the lights turn off and the hologram returns, I turn my attention to the pictures on the walls; there is so much destruction this world made, which is all the more reason why we have to restore it. "Welcome to Eden." The hologram finally disappears, and the last door creaks open once more.

As we reenter Eden, we see the large oak tree in the middle of the open area. The birds singing and flying around ignore us as they mind their own business.

I smile as I look up at James who also is smiling while he looks around Eden once more. I turn to Bex. "James and I decided a while ago we wanted to do an experiment and see if we collected seeds from Eden, if they will survive in the wastelands above."

Bex turns to look to me. "And? Did it work?"

"I planted an acorn about a month ago in New Hampshire, and went back to check on it a few days ago and it is growing, which is a huge step forward to our goals."

Bex seems deep in thought for a moment. "I may know how to help with that. This group I am with, the idea I gave them was to create large scale water purifiers. If we could go around and purify all of the water locations there is a chance we could help these new plants by reducing the amount of nuka rain that might come from those water sources."

"That is an excellent idea, Bex!"

"Once I have a few working prototypes, we can take them to different settlements, so they can purify their water. Over time, we can purify the entire wasteland's water. While also bringing back all of the trees and plants that were lost when the bombs fell."

I look up at James with excitement. We all have a common goal; to fix the world. To do that, we have to start somewhere, and that somewhere is here in Portland.

Chapter 32

The following day, Bex picks up her backpack and throws it into the car she and James had arrived in.

"I wish you did not have to leave." I admit as I hug her tightly.

"I know. I do too. But if we want to have this prototype working, I have to go back to Fort Exodus." She lets out a loud laugh. "I bet you did not expect that to come out of my mouth."

I let out a chuckle. "Definitely not."

"I will come back soon, I promise." With a smile and a wave she drives away to make her way back to Fort Exodus.

James walks up behind me as I watch Bex leave. "Did she just take my car?"

"There are plenty of cars, you will be fine." I chuckle as I turn my attention to him.

"But, I liked that car." He grins, showing me he is joking.

"So, that conversation we were having the other day." I turn to face him.

"What about it?" His smile fades as he looks at me.

"I think, maybe, now that we are alone, would be a good time to take Bex's advice."

He blinks in shock before he grins. "Are you sure about that? She hasn't been known for sound advice."

I roll my eyes at him. "James, shut up and kiss me." I stand up on my tiptoes and kiss him softly on the lips. He wraps his arms around me as he kisses back while holding me tightly in his embrace.

~ ~ ~

The next few weeks, we take the seeds I collected and take some time to plant them all across Maine and even a little ways into New Hampshire. As we are walking back to Portland's Headlight, a call comes to James' radio. We stop a moment for him to answer it.

"Hello? What did you need?"

"Officer James, you are needed in Hawaii. It is top secret and you are required to get here as soon as you can."

"Understood. I will head that way as soon as I can." He turns off his radio and sighs as he looks down at me.

"I knew you would have to leave again, and I am not going to keep you from your orders. I will still be here when you get back."

He holds me close and kisses my forehead. "I wish I could take you with me. I hate protocol."

"So do I, but you heard them. It is top secret. Even if I wanted to, I cannot join you."

We find him a working car and place his bag in the front seat. He holds me close and softly kisses me. I long for this to never end but I know he has to leave. I just hope for not as long as his last trip was.

"I will be back as soon as I can." He leans out of the car window to kiss me once more.

"I will be here." I smile and wave as he drives away quickly. *I should have told him to not drive like a maniac.* I shake my head and concentrate on remembering the feeling of his kiss and his embrace as long as I can.

The night is quiet and a bit lonely, having gotten comfortable with James' presence here, it is hard to go back to just Kota and myself. I sleep on the couch, my room too far away from the door. Without the others, I feel safer here.

In the morning, I pull on my backpack full of supplies as well as my sword. I look out the window and notice the fog-cover and smile. Perfect day to start planting more seeds. With New Hampshire and Maine covered, it is time to make my way farther away.

I shove the map into my coat pocket. With Kota by my side, panting, happily awaiting our next adventure, we will go south to Florida and then work our way slowly back up, one state at a time.

The sun begins to creep through the fog as we begin our walk south, but we instantly stop the moment I hear what sounds like a helicopter coming from behind me. I look from Portland's Headlight to where this helicopter slices through the fog as it is preparing to land in Portland. It seems my new adventure to Florida will have to wait. A different adventure has just found me.

I grin widely as I take my sword out and hold it up, ready to fight whomever these people are that are now exiting the helicopter and making their way towards me.

Let the games begin.

To be continued……

OTHER BOOKS BY E.C. YOHO

CRESSWORTH AND LOCKWOOD SERIES
GENERA-MYSTERY

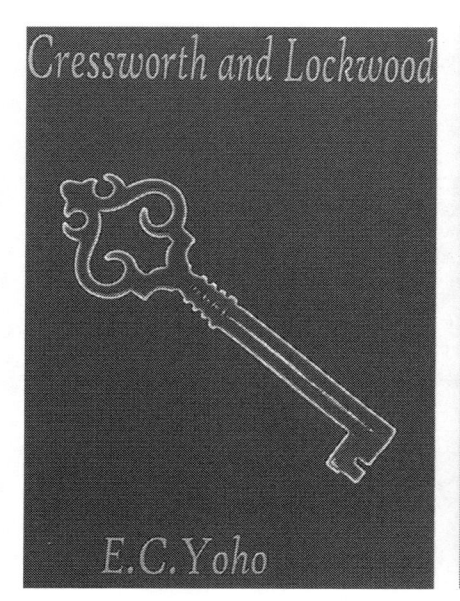

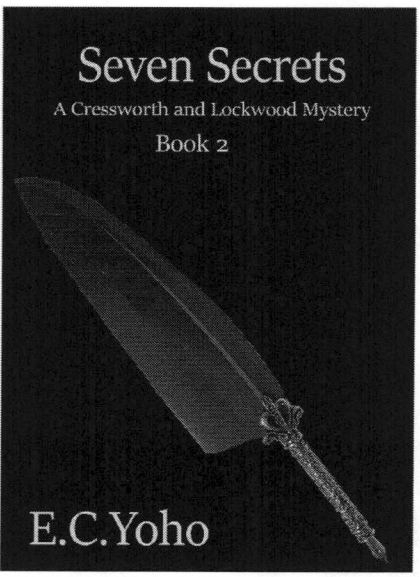

About the Author

E.C. Yoho, originally from a small town in British Columbia, now lives in Northeastern Ohio with her husband and two very spoiled cats.

E.C. always loved to write, but did not consider becoming an author until she was driving to work one day and was rear ended. Writing became an escape that she loved, and ever since then that is all she wants to do.

Sharing her work, she hopes you will find entertainment, humor and just enjoy entering a world where her character's will grow and evolve in more ways than you could imagine.

Her book genres are Mystery, Historical Fiction, and Science Fiction. Most currently still in the works but will be coming out soon.

Follow E.C. Yoho On

Also available on Kindle

Made in the USA
Columbia, SC
09 February 2024

2303903d-d3d0-4cc5-a135-fab1282778d1R01